A MARCH OF KINGS

(BOOK #2 IN THE SORCERER'S RING)

MORGAN RICE

ISBN: 978-1-939416-05-6

Books by Morgan Rice

THE SURVIVAL TRILOGY
ARENA ONE (BOOK #1)
ARENA TWO (BOOK #2)

the Vampire Legacy
resurrected (book #1)
craved (book #2)

the Vampire Journals
turned (book #1)
loved (book #2)
betrayed (book #3)
destined (book #4)
desired (book #5)
betrothed (book #6)
vowed (book #7)
found (book #8)

"Is this a dagger which I see before me,
The handle toward my hand?
Come, let me clutch thee.
I have thee not, and yet I see thee still."

—William Shakespeare, *Macbeth*

CHAPTER ONE

King MacGil stumbled into his chamber, having had way too much to drink, the room spinning and his head pounding from the night's festivities. A woman whose name he did not know clung to his side, one arm draped around his waist, her shirt half-removed, leading him with a giggle towards his bed. Two attendants closed the door behind them and disappeared discreetly.

MacGil did not know where his queen was, and on this night he did not care. They rarely shared a bed anymore, she often retiring to her own chamber, especially on nights of feasts, when the meals went on too long. She knew of her husband's indulgences, and she did not seem to care. After all, he was king, and MacGil kings had always ruled with entitlement.

But as MacGil aimed for bed the room spun too fiercely, and he suddenly threw this woman off. He was no longer in the mood for this.

"Leave me!" he commanded, and shoved her away.

The woman stood there, stunned and hurt, and the door opened and the attendants returned, each grabbing one arm and leading her out. She protested, but her cries were muffled as they closed the door behind her.

MacGil sat on the edge of his bed and rested his head in his hands, trying to get his headache to stop. It was unusual for him to have a headache this early, before the drink had time to wear off, but tonight was different. It had all changed so quickly. The feast had been going so well; he had been settling in with a fine choice of meat, a strong cask of wine, when that boy, Thor, had to surface and ruin everything. First it was his intrusion, with his silly dream; then his knocking his goblet out of his hands.

Then that dog had to appear and lap it up, and drop dead in front of everyone. MacGil had been shaken ever since. The realization had stuck him like a hammer: someone had tried to poison him. To assassinate him. He could hardly process it. Someone had snuck past his guards, past his wine and food tasters. He had been a breath away from being dead, and it still shook him.

He recalled Thor's being taken away, to the dungeon, and he wondered again if it had been the right command. On the one hand, of course, there was no way the boy could have known that goblet was poisoned unless he himself had poisoned it, or was somehow complicit in the crime. On the other hand, he knew Thor had deep, mysterious powers, too mysterious, and perhaps he had been telling the truth: maybe he had indeed envisioned it in a dream. Maybe he had, in fact, saved his life, and maybe MacGil had sent to the dungeon the one person truly loyal.

MacGil's head pounded at the thought, as he sat there rubbing his too-lined forehead, trying to work it all out. But he had drank too much on this night, his mind was too foggy, his thoughts swirled, and he could not get to the bottom of it all. It was too hot in here, a sultry summer night, his body overheated with hours of food and drink, and he felt himself sweating.

He reached over and threw off his mantle, then his outer shirt, dressed in nothing but his undershirt, and reached up and wiped the sweat off his brow, then his beard. He leaned back and pulled off his huge, heavy boots, one at a time, and curled his toes as they hit the air. He sat there and breathed hard, trying to regain his equilibrium. His belly had grown today, and it was burdensome. He kicked his legs up and lay back, resting his head on the pillow. He sighed and looked up, past the four posters, to the ceiling, and tried to get the room to stop spinning.

Who would want to kill him? he wondered, yet again. He had loved that boy, Thor, like a son, and a part of him sensed that it could not be him. He wondered who else it could be, what motive he might have—and most importantly, if he would try again. Was he safe? Had Argon's pronouncements been right?

MacGil felt his eyes grow heavy, as he sensed the answer just outside of his mind's grasp. If his mind was just a little clearer, maybe he could work it all out. But his mind was not there. He would have to wait for the light of morning to summon his advisers, to launch an investigation. The question in his mind was not who wanted him dead—but who did *not* want him dead. His court, he knew, was filled with people who craved his throne. Ambitious generals; maneuvering councilmembers; power-hungry nobles and lords; spies; old rivals; assassins from the McClouds— and maybe even from the Wilds. Perhaps, even closer than that.

MacGil's eyes fluttered as he began to fall into sleep; but something caught his attention which kept them open. He detected movement, and looked over to see that his attendants were not there. He blinked, confused. His attendants never left him alone. In fact, he could not remember the last time he had been alone in this room, by himself. He did not remember ordering them to leave. Even stranger: his door was wide open.

At the same moment MacGil heard a noise from the far side of the room, and turned and looked. There, creeping along the wall, coming out of the shadows, into the torchlight, was a tall, thin man, wearing a black cloak and hood, pulled over his face. MacGil blinked several times, wondering if he were seeing things. At first he was sure it was just shadows, flickering torchlight playing tricks on his eyes.

But a moment later the figure was several paces closer and approaching his bed quickly. MacGil tried to focus in the dim light, to see who it was; he began instinctively to sit up, and being the old warrior he was, he reached for his waist, for a sword, or at least a dagger. But he had undressed long ago, and there were no weapons to be had. He sat, unarmed, on his bed.

The figure moved quickly now, like a snake in the night, getting ever closer, and as MacGil sat up, he got a look at his face. The room still spun, and his drinking prevented him from seeing clearly, but for a moment, he could have sworn it was the face of his son.

Gareth.

MacGil's heart flooded with sudden panic, as he wondered what he could possibly be doing here, unannounced, so late into the night.

"My son?" he called out.

MacGil saw the deadly intent in his eyes, and it was all he needed to see—he started to jump out of bed.

But the figure moved too quickly. He leapt into action, and before MacGil could raise his hand in defense, there was the gleaming of metal in the torchlight, and fast, too fast, there was a blade puncturing the air—and plunging into his heart.

MacGil shrieked, a deep dark cry of anguish, and was surprised by the sound of his own scream. It was a battle scream, one he had heard too many times. It was the scream of a warrior mortally wounded.

MacGil felt the cold metal breaking through his ribs, pushing through muscle, mixing with his blood, then pushing deeper, ever deeper, the pain more intense than he had ever imagined, as it seemed to never stop plunging. With a great gasp, he felt hot, salty blood fill his mouth, felt his breathing grow hard. He forced himself to look up, at the face behind the hood. He was surprised: he had been wrong. It was not the face of his son. It was someone else. Someone he recognized. He could not remember who, but he knew it was someone close to him. Someone who looked like his son.

His brain wracked with confusion, as he tried to put a name to the face.

As the figure stood over him, holding the knife, MacGil somehow managed to raise a hand and push it into the man's shoulder, trying to get him to stop. He felt a burst of the old warrior's strength rise up within him, felt the strength of his ancestors, felt some deep part of him that made him king, that would not give up. With one giant shove, he managed to push back the assassin with all his might.

The man was thinner, more frail, than MacGil thought, and he went stumbling back with a cry, tripping across the room. MacGil managed to stand, and with a supreme effort, he reached down and yanked the knife from his chest. He threw it across the room and it hit the stone floor with a clang, skidding across it, and slammed into the far wall.

The man, whose hood had fallen back around his shoulders, scrambled to his feet and stared back, wide-eyed with terror, as MacGil began to bear down on him. The man turned and ran across the room, stopping only long enough to grab the dagger before he fled.

MacGil tried to chase him, but the man was too fast, and suddenly the pain rose up, piercing his chest. He felt himself grow weak.

MacGil stood there, alone in the room, and looked down at the blood pouring from his chest, into his open palms. He sank to his knees.

He felt his body grow cold, and leaned back and tried to call out.

"Guards," came his faint cry.

He took a deep breath, and with supreme agony, managed to muster his deep voice. The voice of a once-king.

"GUARDS!" he shrieked.

He heard footsteps come running, from some distant hallway, slowly getting closer. He heard a distant door open, sensed bodies getting closer to him. But the room spun again, and this time it was not from drink.

The last thing he saw was the cold stone floor, rising up to meet his face.

CHAPTER TWO

Thor grabbed the iron knocker of the immense wooden door before him and pulled with all his might. It opened slowly, creaking, and revealed before him the king's chamber. He took a step in, feeling the hairs on his arms tingle as he crossed the threshold. He could feel a great darkness here, lingering in the air like a fog.

Thor took several steps into the chamber, hearing the crackle of the torchlight on the walls as he made his way towards the body, lying in a heap on the floor. He already sensed that it was the king, that he had been murdered, that he, Thor, had been too late. Thor could not help but wonder where all the guards were, why no one was here to rescue him.

Thor's knees grew weak as he took the final steps to the body; he knelt on the stone, grabbed his shoulder, already cold, and pulled.

There was MacGil, his former king, lying there, eyes wide open, a knife plunged into his chest. It sat there, rigid, like a sword thrust into a stone.

Thor looked up and suddenly saw the king's attendant standing over him. He held a large, bejeweled goblet, the one that Thor recognized from the feast, made of solid gold and covered in rows of rubies and sapphires, and he reached out, while staring at Thor, and poured it slowly onto the king's chest. The wine splashed all over Thor's face.

Thor heard a screeching, and turned to see his falcon, Ephistopheles, perched on the king's shoulder; she licked the wine off his cheek.

Thor heard a noise and turned to see Argon, standing over him, looking down sternly. In one hand he held the crown, shining. In another, his staff.

Argon walked over and placed the crown firmly on Thor's head. Thor could feel it, its weight digging in, fitting snugly, its metal hugging his temples. He looked up at Argon in wonder.

"You are King now," Argon pronounced.

Thor blinked, and when he opened his eyes, before him stood all the members of the Legion, of the Silver, hundreds of men and boys crammed together into the chamber, all facing him. As one, they all knelt, then bowed down to him, their faces low to the ground.

"Our King," came a chorus of voices.

Thor woke with a start. He sat upright, breathing hard, looking all about him. It was dark in here, and humid, and he realized he was sitting on a stone floor, his back to the wall. He squinted in the darkness, saw iron bars in the distance, and beyond them, a flickering torch. Then he remembered: the dungeon. He had been dragged down here, after the feast.

He remembered that guard, punching him in the face, and realized he must have been out, he didn't know how long. He sat up, breathing harder, trying to wash away the horrific dream. It had seemed so real. He prayed that it wasn't true, that the king wasn't dead. The image of that dagger in his chest stuck in his mind. Had Thor really saw something? Or was it all just his imagination?

Thor felt someone kick him on the sole of his foot, and looked up to see a figure standing over him.

"It's about time you woke up," came the voice. "I'm waiting hours."

In the dim light Thor made out the face of a teenage boy, about his age. He was thin, short, with hollow cheeks and pockmarked skin—yet there seemed to be something kind and intelligent behind his green eyes.

"I'm Merek," he said. "Your cellmate. What you in for?"

Thor sat upright, trying to get his wits about him. He leaned back against the wall, ran his hands through his hair, and tried to remember, to piece it all together.

"They say you tried to kill the king," Merek continued.

"He did try to kill him, and we're going to tear him to pieces if he ever gets out from behind those bars," snarled a voice.

A chorus of clanking erupted, tin cups banging against metal bars, and Thor looked to see the entire corridor filled with cells, grotesque-looking prisoners sticking their heads to the bars and, in the flickering torchlight, sneering out at him. Most were unshaven, with missing teeth, and some looked as if they'd been down here for years. It was a horrifying sight, and Thor forced himself to look away. Was he really down here? Would he be stuck down here, with these people, forever?

"Don't worry about them," Merek said. "It's just you and me in this cell. They can't get in. And I could care less if you poisoned the king. I'd like to poison him myself."

"I didn't poison the King," Thor said, indignant. "I didn't poison anyone. I was trying to save him. All I did was knock over his goblet."

"And how did you know the goblet was poisoned?" screamed a voice from down the aisle, eavesdropping. "Magic, I suppose?"

Their came a chorus of cynical laughter from up and down the cell corridor.

"He's psychic!" one of them yelled out, mocking.

The others laughed.

"No, it was just a lucky guess!" another bellowed, to the delight of the others.

Thor glowered, resenting the accusations, wanting to set them all straight. But he knew it would be a waste of time. Besides, he didn't have to defend himself to these criminals.

Merek studied him, with a look that was not as skeptical as the others. He looked as if he were debating.

"I believe you," he said, quietly.

"You do?" Thor asked.

Merek shrugged.

"After all, if you're going to poison the King, would you really be so stupid to let him know?"

Merek turned and walked away, a few paces over to his side of the cell, and leaned back against the wall and sat down, facing Thor.

Now Thor was curious.

"What are *you* in for?" he asked.

"I'm a thief," Merek answered, somewhat proudly.

Thor was taken aback; he'd never been in the presence of a thief before, a *real* thief. He himself had never thought of stealing, and he had always been amazed to realize that some people did.

"Why do you do it?" Thor asked.

Merek shrugged.

"My family has no food. They have to eat. I don't have any schooling, or any skills of any kind. Stealing is what I know. Nothing major. Just food mostly. Whatever gets them through. I got away with it for years. Then I got caught. This is my third time caught, actually. Third time's the worst."

"Why?" Thor asked.

Merek was quiet, then slowly shook his head. Thor could see his eyes well up with tears.

"The king's law is strict. No exceptions. Third offense, they take your hand."

Thor was horrified. He glanced down at Merek's hands; they were both there.

"They haven't come for me yet," Merek said. "But they will."

Thor felt terrible. Merek looked away, as if ashamed, and Thor did, too, not wanting to think about it.

Thor put his head in his hands, his head killing him, trying to piece together his thoughts. The last few days felt like a whirlwind; he could hardly believe how much had happened, so quickly. On the one hand, he felt a sense of success, of vindication: he'd seen the future, had seen MacGil's poisoning, and had saved him from it. Perhaps fate, after all, could be changed, perhaps destiny could be bent. Thor felt a sense of pride: he had saved his king.

On the other hand, here he was, in the dungeon, unable to clear his name. All his hopes and dreams were shattered, any chance of joining the Legion gone. Now he would be lucky if he didn't spend the rest of his days down here. It pained him to think that MacGil, who had taken Thor in like a father, the only real father he had ever had, thought Thor actually tried to kill him. It pained him to think that Reese, his best friend, might believe that he'd tried to kill his father. Or even worse, Gwendolyn. He thought of their last encounter, of her thinking he frequented the brothels, and felt as if everything good in his life had been pulled out from under him. He wondered why this was all happening to him. After all, he had only wanted to do good.

Thor didn't know what would become of him; he didn't care. All he wanted now was to clear his name, for people to know that he hadn't tried to hurt the king; that he had genuine powers, that he really saw the future. He didn't know what would become of him, but he knew one thing: he had to get out of here. Somehow.

Before Thor could finish the thought, he heard footsteps, heavy boots clomping their way down the stone corridors; there came a rattling of keys, and moments later, there came into view a burly jail keeper, the man who had dragged Thor here and punched him in the face. At the sight of him Thor felt the pain well up on his cheek, felt aware of it for the first time, and felt a physical revulsion.

"Well, if it isn't the little pip who tried to kill the King," the warder scowled, as he turned the iron key in the lock. After several reverberating clicks, he reached over and slid back the cell door. He carried shackles in one hand, and a small axe hung from his waist.

"You'll get yours," he sneered at Thor, then turned to Merek, "but now it's your turn, you little thief. Third time," he said with a malicious smile, "no exceptions."

He suddenly dove for Merek, grabbed him roughly, yanked one arm behind his back, clamped down the shackle, then clamped the other end into a hook on the wall. Merek screamed out, tugging wildly against the shackle, trying to break free; but it was useless. The warder got behind him and grabbed him, held him in a bear hug, took his free arm, and placing it down on a stone ledge.

"This will teach you not to steal," he snarled.

He reached back, removed the axe, and raised it high above his head, his mouth open wide, his ugly teeth sticking out as he snarled.

"NO!" Merek screamed.

Thor sat there, horrified, transfixed as their warder brought down his weapon, aiming for Merek's wrist. Thor realized that in moments, this poor boy's hand would be chopped off, forever, for no other reason than his petty thievery for food, to help feed his family. The injustice of it burned inside him, and he knew that he could not allow it. It just wasn't fair.

Thor felt his entire body growing hot, and then felt a burning inside, rising up from his feet and coursing through his palms. He didn't know what was happening to him, but he felt time slow down, felt himself moving faster than the man, felt every instant of every second, as the man's axe hung there in mid-air. Thor felt a burning energy ball in his palm, and reached back and hurled it at his warder.

He watched in amazement as a yellow ball went flying from his palm, through the air, lighting up the dark cell as it left a trail—and went right for the warder's face. It hit him in his head, and as it did, he dropped his axe and went flying across the cell, smashing into a wall and collapsing. Thor saved Merek a split second before the blade reached his wrist.

Merek looked over at Thor, wide-eyed.

The warder shook his head and began to rise, to head for Thor. But Thor felt the power burning through him, and as the warder reached his feet and faced him, Thor ran forward, jumped into the air, and kicked him in the chest. He felt a power he had never known rush through his body, and heard a cracking noise, as his kick sent the large man flying back through the air, smashing against the wall, and down into a heap on the floor, truly unconscious this time.

Merek stood there, shocked, and Thor knew exactly what he had to do. He grabbed the axe, hurried over, held his shackle up against the stone, and chopped it. A great spark flew through the air, as the chain-link was severed. Merek flinched, then raised his head and looked at the chain dangling down to his feet, and realized he was free.

He stared back at Thor, open-mouthed.

"I don't know how to thank you," Merek said. "I don't know how you did that, whatever it is, or who you are—or *what* you are—but you saved my life. I owe you one. And that is something I do not take lightly."

"You owe me nothing," Thor said.

"Wrong," Merek said, reaching out and clasping Thor's forearm. "You're my brother now. And I will repay you. Somehow. Someday."

With that, Merek turned, hurried out the open cell door, and ran down the corridor, to the shouts of the other prisoners.

Thor looked over, saw the unconscious guard, the open cell door, and knew he had to act, too. The shouts of prisoners were growing louder.

Thor stepped out, looked both ways, and decided to run the opposite way of Merek. After all, they couldn't catch them both at once.

CHAPTER THREE

Thor ran through the night, through the chaotic streets of King's Court, amazed at the commotion around him. The streets were more crowded than ever, throngs of people hurrying about in an agitated stir. Many carried torches, lighting up the night, casting stark shadows on faces, while the castle bells tolled incessantly. It was a low ring, coming once a minute, and Thor knew what that meant: death. Death bells. And there was only one person in the kingdom for whom the bells would toll on this night: the king.

Thor's heart pounded as he wondered. He saw that dagger from his dream flash before his eyes. Had it been true?

He had to know for sure. He reached out and grabbed a passerby, a boy running the opposite direction.

"Where are you going?" Thor demanded. "What is all this commotion?"

"Haven't you heard?" the boy shot back, frantic. "Our king is dying. Stabbed. Mobs are forming outside King's Gate, trying to get the news. If it's true, it's terrible for us all. Can you imagine? A land without a king?"

With that, the boy shoved Thor's hand off and turned and ran back into the night.

Thor stood there, his heart pounding, not wanting to acknowledge the reality all around him. He could hardly believe it. His dreams, his premonitions—they were more than fancies. He had seen the future. Twice. And that scared him. His powers were deeper than he knew, and seemed to be getting stronger with each passing day. Where would this all lead?

Thor stood there, trying to figure out where to go next. He had escaped, but now he had no idea where to turn. Surely within moments the royal guards—and possibly all of King's Court—would be out looking out for him. The fact that Thor escaped would just make him seem more guilty. But then again, the fact that MacGil was stabbed while Thor was in prison—wouldn't that vindicate him? Or would it make him seem like part of a conspiracy?

Thor couldn't take any chances. Clearly, the kingdom wasn't in the mood to hear rational thought—it seemed that everyone around him was out for blood. And he would probably be the scapegoat. He needed to find shelter, some place to go where he could ride out the storm and clear his name. The safest place to go, he knew, would be far from here. He should flee, take refuge in his village—or even farther, as far from here as he could get.

But Thor did not want to take the safest route; it was not who he was. He wanted to stay here, to clear his name, and to keep his position in the Legion. He was not a coward, and he did not run.

Most of all, he wanted to see MacGil before he died, assuming he was still alive. He *needed* to see him. He felt overwhelmed with guilt that he hadn't been able to stop the assassination. Why had he been doomed to see the king's death if there was nothing he could do about it? And why had he envisioned him being poisoned when he was, in fact, stabbed?

As Thor stood there, debating, it came to him: Reese. Reese was the one person he could trust not to turn him into the authorities, maybe even to give him safe harbor. He sensed that Reese would believe him. He knew that Thor's love for his father was genuine, and if anyone had a chance of clearing Thor's name, it would be Reese. He had to find him.

Thor took off at a sprint through the back alleys, twisting and turning against the crowd, as he ran away from King's Gate, towards the castle. He knew where Reese's room was—on the eastern wing, close to the outer city wall—and he only hoped that Reese was inside. If he was, maybe he could catch his attention, help him find a way into the castle. Thor had a sinking feeling that if he lingered here, in the streets, he would soon be recognized. And when this mob recognized him, it would tear him to bits.

As Thor turned down street after street, his feet slipping in the mud of the cool summer night, he finally reached the stone wall of the outer ramparts. He stuck close, running alongside it, just beneath the eyes of the watchful soldiers who stood every few feet.

As he neared Reese's window, he reached down and picked up a smooth rock. Luckily, the one weapon they had forgotten to strip him of was his old, trusted sling, and he extracted it from his waist, placed the stone, reached back, and hurled it.

With his flawless aim, Thor managed to send the stone flying over the castle wall and perfectly into the open-air window of Reese's room. Thor heard the stone clack into the inner wall, then waited, ducking low along the wall to escape detection by the King's guards, who flinched at the noise.

Nothing happened for several moments, and Thor's heart dropped, as he wondered if Reese was not in his room after all. If not, Thor would have to flee this place; there was no other way for him to gain safe harbor. He held his breath, his heart pounding, as he waited, watching the opening by Reese's window.

After what felt like an eternity, Thor was about to turn away, when he saw a figure lean his head out the window, brace both palms on the windowsill, and look around with a puzzled expression.

Thor stood, darting out several steps away from the wall, and waved one arm high.

Reese looked down and noticed him. Reese's face lit up in recognition, visible in the torchlight even from here, and, Thor was relieved to see joy on his face. That told him all he needed to know: Reese would not turn him in.

Reese signaled for him to wait, and Thor hurried back to the wall, squatting low just as a guard turned his way.

Thor waited for he did not know how long, ready at any moment to flee from the guards, until finally Reese appeared, bursting through a door in the outer wall, breathing hard as he looked both ways and spotted Thor.

Reese hurried over and embraced him. Thor was overjoyed. He heard a squeaking, and looked down to see, to his delight, Krohn, bundled up in Reese's shirt. Krohn nearly jumped out of the shirt as Reese reached down and handed him to Thor.

Krohn leapt into Thor's arms as Thor hugged him back, whining and squealing and licking Thor's face.

Reese smiled.

"When they took you away, he tried to follow you, and I took him to make sure he was safe."

Thor clasped Reese's forearm, in appreciation. Then he laughed, as Krohn kept licking him.

"I missed you too, boy," Thor laughed, kissing him back. "Quiet now, or the guards will hear us."

Krohn quieted, as if he understood.

"How did you escape?" Reese asked, surprised.

Thor shrugged. He did not quite know what to say. He still felt uncomfortable speaking about his powers, which he did not understand. He didn't want others to think of him as some kind of freak.

"I got lucky I guess," he responded. "I saw an opportunity and I took it."

"I'm amazed a mob did not tear you apart," Reese said.

"It's dark," Thor said. "I don't think anyone recognized me. Not yet, anyway."

"Do you know that every soldier in the kingdom is looking for you? Do you know that my father has been stabbed?"

Thor nodded, serious. "Is he okay?"

Reese's face fell.

"No," he answered, grim. "He is dying."

Thor felt devastated, as if it were his own father.

"You know I had nothing to do with it, don't you?" Thor asked, hopeful. He didn't care what anyone else thought, but he needed his best friend, MacGil's youngest son, to know that he was innocent.

"Of course," Reese said. "Or else I would not be standing here."

Thor felt a wave of relief, and clasped Reese on the shoulder gratefully.

"But the rest of the kingdom will not be so trusting as I," Reese added. "The safest place for you is far from here. I will give you my fastest horse, a pack of supplies, and send you far away. You must hide out, until this all dies down, until they find the true killer. No one is thinking clearly now."

Thor shook his head.

"I cannot leave," he said. "That would make me seem guilty. I need others to know I did not do this. I cannot run from my troubles. I must clear my name."

Reese shook his head.

"If you stay here, they'll find you. You'll get imprisoned again—and then executed—if not killed by a mob first."

"That is a chance I must take," Thor said.

Reese stared at him long and hard, and his look changed from one of concern to one of admiration. Finally, slowly, he nodded.

"You are proud. And stupid. Very stupid. That is why like you."

Reese smiled. Thor smiled back.

"I need to see your father," Thor said. "I need to have a chance to explain to him, face-to-face, that it wasn't me, that I'd nothing to do with it. If he decides to sentence me, then so be it. But I need one chance. I want him to know. That is all I ask of you."

Reese stared back earnestly, summing up his friend. Finally, after what felt like an eternity, he nodded.

"I can get you to him. I know a back way. It leads to his chamber. It's risky—and once you're in, you will be on your own. There is no way out. They'll be nothing I can do for you then. It could mean your death. Are you sure you want to take that chance?"

Thor nodded back with deadly seriousness.

"Very well then," Reese said, and suddenly reached down and threw a cloak at Thor.

Thor caught it and looked down in surprise; he realized Reese must have planned for this all along.

Reese smiled as Thor looked up.

"I knew you'd be dumb enough to want to stay. I'd expect nothing less from my best friend."

CHAPTER FOUR

Gareth paced his chamber, reliving the events of the night, flooded with anxiety. He could hardly believe what had happened at the feast, how it had all gone so wrong. He could hardly comprehend that that stupid boy, that outsider, Thor, had somehow caught onto his poison plot—and even more, had managed to actually intercept the goblet. Gareth thought back to that moment when he saw Thor jump up, knock down the goblet, when he heard the goblet hit the stone, watched the wine spill out on the floor, and saw all his dreams and aspirations spill out with it.

In that moment, he had been ruined. Everything he'd lived for had been crushed. And when that dog lapped up the wine and dropped dead—he knew he was finished. He saw his whole life flash before him, saw himself discovered, sentenced to life in the dungeon for trying to kill his father. Or worse, executed. It was stupid. He should have never gone through with the plan, never visited that witch.

Gareth had, at least, acted quickly, taking a chance and jumping to his feet and being the first to pin the blame on Thor. Looking back, he was proud of himself, at how quickly he had reacted. It had been a moment of inspiration, and to his amazement, it seemed to have worked. They had dragged Thor off, and afterwards, the feast had nearly settled down again. Of course, nothing was the same after that, but at the very least, the suspicion seemed to fall squarely on the boy.

Gareth only prayed that it stayed that way. It had been decades since an assassination attempt on a MacGil, and Gareth feared there would be an inquiry, that they would end up looking more deeply into the deed. Looking back, it had been foolish to try to poison him. His father was invincible. He should have known that. He had over-reached. And now he could not help feel as if it were only a matter of time until the suspicion fell on him. He would have to do whatever he could to prove Thor's guilt, and have him executed before it was too late.

At least Gareth had somewhat redeemed himself: after that failed attempt, he had called off the assassination. Now, Gareth felt relieved. After watching the plot fail, he had realized that there was a part of him, deep down, that did not want to kill his father after all, that did not want to have his blood on his hands. He would not be King. He might never be king. But after tonight's events, that was okay with him. At least he would be free. He could never handle the stress of going through all of this again, the secrets, the covering up, the constant anxiety of being found out. It was too much for him.

As he paced and paced, the night growing late, finally, slowly, he began to calm. Just as he was beginning to feel himself, preparing to settle in for the night, there came a sudden crash, and he turned to see his door burst open. In burst Firth, wide-eyed, frantic, rushing into the room as if he were being chased.

"He's dead!" Firth screamed. "He's dead! I killed him. He's dead!"

Firth was hysterical, wailing, and Gareth had no idea what he was talking about. Was he drunk?

Firth ran throughout the room, shrieking, crying, holding up his hands—and it was then that Gareth noticed his palms, covered in blood, his yellow tunic, stained red.

Gareth's heart skipped a beat. Firth had just killed someone. But who?

"*Who* is dead?" Gareth demanded. "Who do you speak of?"

But Firth was hysterical, and could not focus. Gareth ran to him, grabbed his shoulders firmly and shook him.

"Answer me!"

Firth opened his eyes and stared, with the eyes of a wild horse.

"Your father! The King. He's dead! By my hand!"

At his words, Gareth felt as if a knife had been plunged into his own heart.

He stared back, wide-eyed, frozen, feeling his whole body go numb. He released his grip, took a step back, and tried to catch his breath. He could see from all the blood that Firth was genuine. He could not even fathom it. Firth? The stable boy? The most weak-willed of all his friends? Killed his father?

"But…how is that possible?" Gareth gasped. "When?"

"It happened in his chamber," Firth said. "Just now. I stabbed him."

The reality of the news began to sink in, and Gareth regained his wits; he noticed his open door, ran to it, and slammed it shut, checking first to make sure no guards had seen. Luckily, the corridor was empty. He pulled the heavy iron bolt across it.

He hurried back across the room. Firth was still hysterical, and he needed to calm him. He needed answers.

He grasped him by the shoulders, spun him, and back-handed him hard enough to make him stop. Finally, Firth focused on him.

"Tell me everything," Gareth ordered coldly. "Tell me exactly what happened. Why did you do this?"

"What do you mean why?" Firth asked, confused. "You wanted to kill him. Your poison didn't work. I thought I could help you. I thought that was what you wanted."

Gareth shook his head. He grabbed Firth by the shirt and shook him, again and again.

"Why did you do this!?" Gareth screamed.

Gareth felt his whole world crumbling. He was shocked to realize that he actually felt remorse for his father. He could not understand it. Just hours ago, he'd wanted more than anything to see him poisoned, dead at the table. Now the idea of his being killed struck him like the death of a best friend. He felt overwhelmed with remorse. A part of him had not wanted him to die after all—especially not this way. Not by Firth's hand. And not by a blade.

"I don't understand," Firth whined. "Just hours ago you tried to kill him yourself. Your goblet plot. I thought you would be grateful!"

To his own surprise, Gareth reached back and smacked Firth across the face.

"I did not tell you to do this!" Gareth spat. "I *never* told you to do this. Why did you kill him? Look at you. You are covered in blood. Now we are both finished. It is only a matter of time until the guards catch us."

"No one saw," Firth pleaded. "I slipped between the shifts. No one spotted me."

"And where is the weapon?"

"I did not leave it," Firth said proudly. "I'm not stupid. I disposed of it."

"And what blade did you use?" Gareth asked, his mind spinning with the implications. He went from remorse to worry; his mind raced with every detail of the trail that this bumbling fool might have left, every detail that might lead to him.

"I used one that could not be traced," Firth said, proud of himself. "It was a dull, anonymous blade. I found it in the stables. There were four others just like it. It could not be traced," he repeated.

Gareth felt his heart drop.

"Was it a short knife, with a red handle and a curved blade? Mounted on the wall beside my horse?"

Firth nodded back, looking doubtful.

Gareth glowered.

"You fool. Of course that blade is traceable!"

"But there were no markings on it!" Firth protested, sounding scared, his voice trembling.

"There are no markings on the blade—but there is a mark on the hilt!" Gareth yelled. "Underneath! You did not check carefully. You fool," Gareth said, stepping forward, reddening. "The emblem of my horse is carved underneath it. Anyone who knows the royal family well can trace that blade back to me."

He stared at Firth, who seemed stumped. He wanted to kill him.

"What did you do with it?" Gareth pressed. "Tell me you have it on you. Tell me that you brought it back with you. Please."

Firth swallowed.

"I disposed of it carefully. No one will ever find it."

Gareth grimaced.

"Where, exactly?"

"I threw it down the stone chute, into the castle's chamber pot. They dump the pot every hour, into the river. Do not worry, my lord. It's deep in the river by now."

The castle bells suddenly tolled, and Gareth turned and ran to the open window, his heart flooded with panic. He looked out and saw all the chaos and commotion below, mobs surrounding the castle. Those bells tolling could only mean one thing: Firth was not lying. He had killed his father. He could scarcely believe it.

Gareth felt his body grow icy cold. He could not conceive that he had set in motion such a great evil. And that Firth, of all people, had executed it.

There came a sudden pounding at his door, and as it burst open, several royal guards rushed in. For a moment, Gareth was sure they would arrest him.

But to his surprise, they stopped and stood at attention.

"My Lord, your father has been stabbed. There may be an assassin on the loose. Be sure to stay safe in your room. He is gravely injured."

The hair rose on the back of Gareth's neck at that last word.

"Injured?" Gareth echoed, the word nearly sticking in his throat. "Is he still alive then?"

"He is, my lord. And god be with him, he will survive, and tell us who did this heinous act."

With a short bow the guard hurried from the room, slamming closed the door.

A rage overwhelmed Gareth and he grabbed Firth by his shoulders, drove him across the room and slammed him into a stone wall.

Firth stared back, wide-eyed, looking horrified, speechless.

"What have you done?" Gareth screamed. "Now we are both finished!"

"But…but…." Firth stumbled, "…I was sure he was dead!"

"You are sure of a lot of things," Gareth said, "and they are all wrong!"

A thought occurred to Gareth.

"That dagger," he said. "We have to retrieve it, before it's too late."

"But I threw it away, my lord," Firth said. "It is washed away in the river!"

"You threw it into a chamber pot. That does not mean it is yet in the river."

"But it most likely is!" Firth said.

Gareth could stand this idiot's bumbling no longer. He burst past him, running out the door, Firth on his heels.

"I will go with you. I will show you exactly where I threw it," Firth said.

Gareth stopped in the corridor, turned and stared at Firth. He was covered in blood, and Gareth was amazed the guards had not spotted it. It was lucky. He was more of a liability than ever.

"I'm only going to say this once," Gareth growled. "Get back to my room at once, change your clothes, and burn them. Get rid of any traces of blood. Then disappear from this castle. Stay away from me on this night. Do you understand me?"

Gareth shoved him back, then turned and ran. He sprinted down the corridor, ran down the spiral stone staircase, going down level after level, towards the servant's quarters.

Finally, he burst into the basement, to the turned heads of several servants. They had been in the midst of scrubbing enormous pots and boiling pails of water. Huge fires roared amidst brick kilns, and the servants, wearing stained aprons, were drenched in sweat.

On the far side of the room Gareth spotted an enormous chamber pot, filth hailing down from a chute and splashing in it every minute.

Gareth ran up to the closest servant and grabbed his arm desperately.

"When was the last pot emptied?" Gareth asked.

"It was taken to the river just minutes ago, my lord."

Gareth turned and raced out the room, sprinting down the castle corridors, back up the spiral staircase, and bursting out into the cool night air.

He ran across the grass field, breathless as he sprinted for the river.

As he neared it, he found a place to hide, behind a large tree, close to the shore. He watched two servants raise the huge iron pot and tilt it into the rushing current of the river.

He watched until it was upside down, all of its contents emptied, until they turned back with the pot and trekked back towards the castle.

Finally, Gareth was satisfied. No one had spotted any blade. Wherever it was, it was now in the river's tides, being washed away into anonymity. If his father should die on this night, there would be no evidence left to trace the murderer.

Or would there?

CHAPTER FIVE

Thor followed on Reese's heels, Krohn behind him as they weaved their way through the back passageway to his father's chamber. Reese had brought him through a secret door, hidden in one of the stone walls, and as Reese held a torch, they walked single file in the cramped space, working their way through the inner guts of the castle in a dizzying array of twists and turns. They ascended a narrow, stone staircase, which led to another passageway. They turned, and before them was another staircase. Thor marveled at how intricate this passage was.

"This passageway was built into the castle hundreds of years ago," Reese explained in a whisper as they went, breathing hard as he climbed. "It was built by my father's great-grandfather, the third MacGil king. He had it built after a siege—it's an escape route. Ironically, we were never under siege since, and these passageways haven't been used in centuries. They were boarded up and I discovered them years ago. I like to use them from time to time. I can get around the castle and no one knows where I am. When we were younger, Gwen and Godfrey and I would play hide and seek in them. Kendrick was too old, and Gareth didn't like to play with us. No torches, that was the rule. Pitch black. It was terrifying at the time."

Thor tried to keep up as Reese navigated the passage with a stunning display of virtuosity, obvious that he knew every step by heart.

"How do you possibly remember all these turns?" Thor asked in awe.

"You get lonely growing up as a boy in this castle," Reese continued, "especially when everyone else is older, and you're too young to join the Legion, and there's nothing else to do. I made it my mission to discover every nook and cranny of this place."

They turned again, went down three stone steps, turned through a narrow opening in the wall, then went down a long stairwell. Finally, Reese brought them to a thick, oak door, covered in dust. He leaned one ear against it and listened. Thor came up beside him.

"What door is this?" Thor asked

"Shhh," Reese said.

Thor grew quiet, as he hunched over and put his ear against the door, listening. Krohn stood there behind him, looking up.

"It is the back door to my father's chamber," Reese whispered. "I want to hear who's in there with him."

Thor listened, his heart pounding, to the muffled voices behind the door.

"Sounds like the room is full," Reese said.

Reese turned and gave Thor a meaningful look.

"You will be walking into a firestorm. His generals will be there, his council, his advisers, his family—everyone. And I'm sure every one of them will be on the lookout for you, his supposed murderer. It will be like walking into a lynching mob. If my father still thinks you did it, you'll be finished. Are you sure you want to do this?"

Thor swallowed hard. It was now or never. His throat went dry, as he realized this was one of the turning moments of his life. It would be easy to turn back now, to flee. He could live a safe life somewhere, far from King's Court. Or he could pass through that door and potentially spend the rest of his life in the dungeon, with those cretins—or even executed.

He breathed deep, and decided. He had to face his demons head-on. He could not back away.

Thor nodded. He was afraid to open his mouth, afraid that if he did, he might change his mind.

Reese nodded back, with a look of approval, then pushed the iron handle and leaned his shoulder into the door.

Thor squinted in the bright torchlight as the door flew open. He found himself standing in the center of the king's private chamber, Krohn and Reese beside him.

There were at least two dozen people crammed in around the king, who lay on his bed; some stood over him, others knelt. Surrounding the king were his advisers and generals, along with Argon, the Queen, Kendrick, Godfrey—even Gwendolyn. It was a death vigil, and Thor was intruding on his family's private affair.

The atmosphere in the room was somber, the faces grave. MacGil lay propped up on pillows, and

Thor was relieved to see that he was still alive—at least for now.

All the faces turned at once, startled at Thor's and Reese's sudden entrance. Thor realized what a shock it must have been, with their sudden appearance in the middle of the room, coming out of a secret door in the stone wall.

"That's the boy!" someone from the crowd yelled, standing and pointing at Thor with hatred. "He's the one who tried to poison the king!"

Guards bore down on him from all corners of the room. Thor hardly knew what to do. A part of him wanted to turn and flee, but he knew he had to face this angry mob, had to have his peace with the king. So he braced himself, as several guards ran forward, reaching out to grab him. Krohn, at his side, snarled, warning his attackers.

As Thor stood there, he felt a sudden heat rise up within him, a power surging through him; he raised one hand, involuntarily, and held out a palm and directed his energy towards them.

Thor was amazed as they all stopped in mid-stride, feet away, as if frozen. His power, whatever it was, welling within him, kept them at bay.

"How dare you march in here and use your sorcery, boy!" Brom yelled, drawing his sword. "Was trying to kill our king once not enough?"

Brom approached Thor with his sword drawn; as he did, Thor felt something overcome him, a feeling stronger than he'd ever had. He simply closed his eyes and focused. He sensed the energy within Brom's sword, its shape, its metal, and somehow, he became one with it. He willed it to stop in his mind's eye.

Brom stood frozen in his tracks, wide-eyed.

"Argon!" Brom spun and yelled. "Stop this sorcery at once! Stop this boy!"

Argon stepped from the crowd, and slowly lowered his hood. He stared back at Thor with intense, burning eyes.

"I see no reason to stop him," Argon said. "He has not come here to harm."

"Are you mad? He's nearly killed our King!"

"That is what you suppose," Argon said. "That is not what I see."

"Leave him be," came a gravelly, deep voice.

Everyone turned as MacGil sat up. He looked over, very faint. It was clearly a struggle for him to speak.

"I want to see the boy. He is not the one that killed me. I saw the man's face, and it was not him. Thor is innocent."

Slowly, the others relaxed their guard, and Thor relaxed his mind, letting them go. The guards backed away, looking at Thor warily, as if he were from another realm, and slowly put their swords back in their scabbards.

"I want to see him," MacGil said. "Alone. All of you. Leave us."

"My King," Brom said. "Do you really think that is safe? Just you and this boy alone?"

"Thor is not to be touched," MacGil said. "Now leave us. All of you. Including my family."

A thick silence fell over the room as everyone stared at each other, clearly unsure what to do. Thor stood there, rooted in place, hardly able to process at all.

One by one the others, including the King's family, filed from the room, as Krohn left with Reese. The chamber, so filled with people but moments before, suddenly became empty.

The door closed. It was just Thor and the king, alone in the silence. He could hardly believe it. Seeing MacGil lying there, so pale, in such pain, hurt Thor more than he could say. He did not know why, but it was almost as if a part of him were dying there, too, on that bed. He wanted more than anything for the king to be well.

"Come here my boy," MacGil said weakly, his voice hoarse, barely above a whisper.

Thor lowered his head and hurried to the king's side, kneeling before him. He held out a limp wrist, and Thor reached up, took his hand, and kissed it.

Thor looked up and saw MacGil smiling down weakly. Thor was surprised to feel hot tears flooding his own cheeks.

"My liege," Thor began, all in a rush, unable to keep it in, "please believe me. I did not poison you. I knew of the plot only from my dream. From some power of which I know not of. I only wanted to warn you. Please, believe me—"

MacGil held up a palm, and Thor fell silent.

"I was wrong about you," MacGil said. "It took my being killed by another man's hand to realize it wasn't you. You were just trying to save me. Forgive me. You were loyal. Perhaps the only loyal member of my court."

"How I wish I had been wrong," Thor said. "How I wish that you were safe. That my dreams were just illusions; that you were never assassinated. Maybe I was wrong. Maybe you'll survive."

MacGil shook his head.

"My time has come," he said to Thor.

Thor swallowed, hoping it wasn't true but sensing that it was.

"Do you know who did this terrible act, my lord?" Thor asked the question that had been burning through his mind since he'd had the dream. He could not imagine who would want to kill the king, or why.

MacGil looked up at the ceiling, blinking with effort.

"I saw his face. It is a face I know well. But for some reason, I cannot place it."

He turned and looked at Thor.

"It doesn't matter now. My time has come. Whether it was by his hand, or by some other, the end is still the same. What matters now," he said, and reached out and grabbed Thor's wrist with a strength that surprised him, "is what happens after I'm gone. Ours will be a kingdom without a king."

MacGil looked at Thor with an intensity that Thor did not understand. Thor did not know precisely what he was saying, what, if anything, he was demanding of him. He wanted to ask, but he could see how hard it was for him to catch his breath, and did not want to risk interrupting him.

"Argon was right about you," he said, slowly releasing his grip. "Your destiny is far greater than mine."

Thor felt an electric shock through his body at the king's words. His destiny? Greater than the King's? The very idea that the King would even bother to discuss Thor with Argon was more than Thor could comprehend. And the fact that he would say that Thor's destiny was greater than the King's—what could he possibly mean? Was the king just being delusional in his final moments?

"I chose you…I brought you into my family for a reason. Do you know what that reason is?"

Thor shook his head, wanting desperately to know.

"Don't you know why I wanted you here, only you, in my final moments?"

Thor racked his brain, desperately trying to understand. But he had no idea.

"I'm sorry, my liege," he said, shaking his head. "I do not know."

MacGil smiled faintly, as his eyes began to close.

"There is a great land, far from here. Beyond the Wilds. Beyond even the land of the Dragons. It is the land of the Druids. Where your mother is from. You must go there to seek the answers."

MacGil's eyes opened wide and he stared at Thor with an intensity that Thor could not comprehend.

"Our kingdom depends on it," he added. "You are not like the others. You are special. Until you understand who you are, our kingdom will never rest at ease."

MacGil's eyes closed and his breathing grew shallow, each breath coming out with a gasp. His grip slowly weakened on Thor's wrist, and Thor felt his own tears welling up. His mind was spinning with everything the king had said, as he tried to make sense of it all. He could barely concentrate. Had he heard it all correctly?

MacGil began to whisper something, but it was so quiet, Thor could barely make it out. Thor leaned in close, bringing his ear to MacGil's lips.

The king lifted his head one last time, and with one final effort said:

"Avenge me."

Then, suddenly, MacGil stiffened. He lay there for a few moments, then his head rolled to the side as his eyes opened wide, frozen.

Dead.

"NO!" Thor wailed.

His wail must have been loud enough to alert the guards, because a moment later, he heard a door burst open behind him, heard the commotion of dozens of people rushing into the room. In the corner of his consciousness he understood there was motion all around him. He dimly heard the castle bells tolling out, again and again. The bells pounded, matching the pounding of the blood in his temples. But it all became a blur, as moments later the room was spinning, he fainting, heading for the stone floor in one great collapse.

CHAPTER SIX

A gust of wind struck Gareth in the face and he looked up, blinking back tears, into the pale light of the first rising sun. The day was just breaking, and yet at this remote spot, here on the edge of the Kolvian Cliffs, there were already gathered hundreds of the king's family, friends, and close royal subjects, hovering close, hoping to participate in the funeral. Just beyond them, held back by an army of soldiers, Gareth could see the thousands of masses pouring in, watching the services from a distance. The grief on their faces was genuine. His father was loved, that was certain.

Gareth stood with the rest of the immediate family, in a semi-circle around his father's body, which sat suspended on planks over a pit in the earth, ropes around it, waiting to be lowered. Argon stood before the crowd, wearing the deep-scarlet robes he reserved only for funerals, his expression inscrutable as he looked down at the King's body, the hood covering his face. Gareth tried desperately to analyze that face, to decipher how much Argon knew. Did Argon know that he murdered his father? And if so, would he tell the others—or let destiny play out?

To Gareth's bad luck, that annoying boy, Thor, had been cleared of guilt; obviously, he could not have stabbed the king while he was in the dungeon. Not to mention that his father himself had told all the others that Thor was innocent. Which only made things worse for Gareth. A council had already been formed to look into the matter, to scrutinize every detail of his murder. Gareth's heart pounded as he stood there with the others, staring at the body about to be lowered into the earth; he wanted to be lowered with it.

He knew it was only a matter of time until the trail led to Firth—and when it did, he would be brought down with him. He would have to act quickly to divert the attention, to pin the blame on someone else. Gareth wondered if those around him suspected him. He was likely just being paranoid, and as he surveyed the faces, he saw none looking at him. There stood his brothers, Reese, Godfrey, Kendrick, his sister, Gwendolyn, his mother, her face wrought with grief, looking catatonic; indeed, since his father's death, she had been like a different person, barely able to speak. He'd heard that when she'd received the news something had happened within her, some sort of paralysis. Half of her face was frozen; when she opened her mouth, the words came out too slow.

Gareth examined the faces of the King's council behind her—his lead general, Brom and the Legion head, Kolk, stood in front, behind whom stood his father's endless advisers. They all feigned grief, but Gareth knew better. He knew that all of these people, all of the councilmembers and advisers and generals—and all of the nobles and lords behind them—barely cared. He recognized on their faces ambition. Lust for power. As each stared down at his father's corpse, he felt that each wondered who might be next to grab the throne.

It was the very thought that Gareth was having. What would happen in the aftermath of such a chaotic assassination? If it had been clean and simple, and the blame pinned on someone else, then Gareth's plan would have been perfect—the throne would fall to him. After all, he was the first-born, legitimate son. His father had ceded power to Gwendolyn, but no one was present at that meeting except for his siblings, and his wishes were never ratified. Gareth knew the council, and knew how seriously they took the law. Without a ratification, his sister could not rule.

Which, again, led to him. If due process took its course—and Gareth was determined to make sure it did—then the throne would have to fall on him. That was the law.

His siblings would fight him, he had no doubt. They would recall their meeting with their father, and probably insist that Gwendolyn rule. Kendrick would not try to take power for himself—he was too pure-hearted. Godfrey was apathetic; Reese was too young. Gwendolyn was his only real threat. But Gareth was optimistic: he didn't think the council was ready for a woman—much less a teenage girl—to rule the Ring. And without a ratification from the king, they had the perfect excuse to pass her over.

The only real threat left in Gareth's mind was Kendrick. After all, he, Gareth, was universally hated while Kendrick was loved among the common men, among the soldiers. Given the circumstance, there was always the chance of their wanting to hand the throne to Kendrick. The sooner Gareth could take power, the sooner he could use his powers to quash Kendrick.

Gareth felt a tug at his hand, and looked down to see the knotted rope burning his palm. He realized they had begun lowering his father's coffin; he looked over and saw his other siblings, each holding a rope like he, slowly lowering it. Gareth's end tilted, as he was late lowering, and he reached out and grabbed the rope with his other hand until finally it leveled out. It was ironic: even in death, he could not please his father.

Distant bells tolled, coming from the castle, and Argon stepped forward and raised a palm.

"*Itso ominus domi ko resepia…*"

The lost language of the Ring, the royal language, used by his ancestors for a thousand years. It was a language his private tutors had drilled into him as a boy—and one he would need as he assumed his royal powers.

Argon suddenly stopped, looked up, and stared right at Gareth. It sent a chill through Gareth's spine, as Argon's translucent eyes seemed to burn right through him. Gareth's face flushed, and he wondered if the whole kingdom was watching, and if any knew what it meant. In that stare, he felt that Argon knew of his involvement. And yet Argon was mysterious, always refusing to get involved in the twists and turns of human fate. Would he stay quiet?

"King MacGil was a good king, a fair king," Argon said slowly, his voice deep and unearthly. "He brought pride and honor to his ancestors, and riches and peace to this kingdom unlike any we've ever known. His life was taken prematurely, as the Gods would have it. But he left behind a legacy deep and rich. Now it is up to us to fulfill that legacy."

Argon paused.

"Our kingdom of the Ring is surrounded by threats deep and ominous on all sides. Beyond our Canyon, protected only by our energy shield, lie a nation of savages and creatures that would tear us apart. Within our Ring, opposite our Highlands, lies a clan that would do us harm. We live in unmatched prosperity and peace; yet our security is fleeting.

"Why do the gods take someone away from us in his prime—a good and wise and fair king? Why was his destiny to be murdered this way? We are all merely pawns, puppets in fate's hand. Even at the height of our power, we can end up beneath the earth. The question we must grapple with is not what we strive for—but who we strive to be."

Argon lowered his head, and Gareth felt his palms burning as they lowered the coffin all the way; it finally hit the ground with a thud.

"NO!" came a shriek.

It was Gwendolyn. Hysterical, she ran for the edge of the pit, as if to throw herself in; Reese ran forward and grabbed her, held her back. Kendrick stepped up to help.

But Gareth felt no sympathy for her; rather, he felt threatened. If she wanted to be under the earth, he could arrange that.

Yes, indeed, he could.

*

Thor stood just feet away from King MacGil's body as he watched it lowered into the earth, and felt overwhelmed by the site. Perched on the edge of the highest cliff of the kingdom, the king had chosen a spectacular place to be buried, a lofty place, which seemed to reach into the clouds themselves. The clouds were tinged with orange and greens and yellows and pinks, as the first of the rising suns crawled its way higher into the sky. But the day was covered with a mist that would not rise, as if the kingdom itself were mourning. Krohn, beside him, whimpered.

Thor heard a screech, and looked up to see Ephistopheles, circling high above, looking down on them. Thor was still numb; he could hardly believe the events of the last few days, that he was standing here now, in the midst of the king's family, watching this man he had grown so quickly to love be lowered into the earth. It seemed impossible. He had barely begun to know him, the first man that had ever been like a real father, and now he was being taken away. More than anything, Thor could not stop thinking of the king's final words.

You are not like the others. You are special. And until you understand who you are, our kingdom will never rest at ease.

What had he meant by that? Who was he, exactly? How was he special? How did the king know? What did the fate of the kingdom have to do with Thor? Had he just been delirious?

There is a great land, far from here. Beyond the Empire. Beyond even the land of the Dragons. It is the land of the Druids. Where your mother is from. You must go there to seek the answers.

How had MacGil known about his mother? How had he known where she lived? And what sort of answers did she have? Thor could not stop thinking about her. He had always assumed she was dead. The idea that she could be alive electrified him. He felt determined, more than ever, to seek her out, to find her. To find the answers, to discover who he was, why he was special.

As a bell tolled and MacGil's corpse began to lower, Thor wondered about the cruel twists and turns of fate; why had he been allowed to see the future, to see this great man killed—yet made powerless to do anything about it? In some ways, he wished he had never seen any of this, had never known in advance what would happen; he wished he had just been an innocent bystander like the rest, just woken one day to learn that the king was dead. Now he felt as if he were a part of it. Somehow, he felt guilty, as if he should have done more.

Thor wondered what would become of the kingdom now. It was a kingdom without a king. Who would reign? Would it be, as everyone speculated, Gareth? Thor could not imagine anything worse.

Thor scanned the crowd and saw the stern faces of the nobles and lords, gathered here from all corners of the Ring; he knew them to be powerful men, from what Reese had told him, in a restless kingdom. He could not help wondering who the killer could be. In all those faces, it seemed as if everyone were suspect. All of these men would be vying for power. Would the kingdom splinter into parts? Would their forces be at odds with each other? And what would become of he, Thor? And of the Legion? Would it be disbanded? Would the army be disbanded? Would The Silver revolt if Gareth was named king?

And after all that had happened, would the others truly believe that Thor was innocent? Would he be forced to return to his village? He hoped not. He loved everything he had; he wanted more than anything to stay here, in this place, in the Legion. He just wanted everything to be as it was, wanted nothing to change. The kingdom, just days ago, had seemed so substantial, so permanent; MacGil had seemed like he would hold the throne forever. If something so secure, so stable could suddenly collapse—what hope did that leave for the rest of them? Nothing felt permanent to Thor anymore.

Thor's heart broke as he watched Gwendolyn try to jump into the grave with her father. As Reese held her back, attendants came forward and began shoveling the mound of dirt into the pit, while Argon continued his ceremonial chanting. A cloud passed in the sky, blotting out the sun for a moment, and Thor felt a cold wind whip through on this warm summer day. He heard a whining, and looked down and saw Krohn at his feet, looking up.

Thor hardly knew what would become of anything anymore, but he knew one thing: he had to talk to Gwen. He had to tell her how sorry he was, tell her how distraught he was, too, over her father's death, tell her that she was not alone. Even if she decided to never see him again, he had to let her know that he had been falsely accused, that he hadn't done anything in that brothel. He needed a chance, just one chance, to set the record straight, before she dismissed him for good.

As the final shovelful of dirt was thrown on the king and the bells tolled again and again, finally, the crowd rearranged itself: rows of people stretched as far as Thor could see, winding their way along the cliff, each holding a single black rose, lining up to pass the fresh mound of dirt that marked the king's grave. Thor stepped forward, knelt down, and placed his rose on the already growing pile. Krohn whined.

As the crowd began to disperse, people milling about in every direction, Thor noticed Gwendolyn break free from Reese's grip and run, hysterical, away from the grave.

"Gwen!" Reese called out after her.

But she was inconsolable. She cut through the thick mob and ran down a dirt trail along the cliff's edge. Thor could not stand to see her like that; he had to try to speak with her.

Thor burst through the crowd himself, Krohn at his heels, weaving this way and that as the crowd grew thick, trying to follow her trail, to catch up with her. Finally, he broke free from the outskirts and spotted her running, far away from the others.

"Gwendolyn!" he screamed out.

She kept running, and Thor chased after her, running double speed, Krohn yelping alongside him. Thor ran faster and faster, until his lungs burned, and finally, he managed to close the gap between them.

He grabbed one of her arms, stopping her.

She wheeled, her eyes red, flooded with tears, her long hair clinging to her cheeks, and threw his hand off.

"Leave me be!" she screamed. "I don't want to see you! Ever again!"

"Gwendolyn," Thor pleaded, "I did not kill your father. I had nothing to do with his death. He said so himself. Don't you realize that? I was trying to save him, not to hurt him."

She tried to flee, but he held her wrist and did not let her go. He could not let her go—not this time. She struggled against him, but did not try to run anymore. She was too busy, weeping.

"I know you didn't kill him," she said. "But that doesn't make you any better. How dare you come and try to speak with me after you humiliated me in front of all the others? Especially now, of all times."

"But you don't understand. I didn't do anything at that brothel. It was all lies. None of it is true. Someone is trying to slander me."

She narrowed her eyes at him.

"So then are you telling me you did not go to that brothel?"

Thor hesitated, unsure what to say.

"I did. I went with all the others."

"And are you saying you did not enter a room with some strange woman?"

Thor looked down, embarrassed, unsure how to respond.

"I suppose I did, but—"

"No buts," she interrupted. "You admit it then. You're disgusting. I want nothing more to do with you."

Her face transformed from distraught to furious. She stopped her crying, as her expression changed to one of rage. She got very calm, got close to him, and said.

"I never want to see your face. Never again. Do you understand me? I don't know what I was thinking to spend any time with you at all. My mother was right. You are just a commoner. You are beneath me."

Her words stung him to his very soul. He felt as if he'd been stabbed.

He let go of her wrist, took several steps back. Perhaps Alton had been right after all. Perhaps he had just been another plaything for her.

He turned without another word and headed away from her, Krohn at his side, and for the first time since he had arrived, he wondered if there were anything left for him here.

CHAPTER SEVEN

Gwendolyn stood there, at the edge of the cliff, watching Thor walk away, and feeling more torn apart by anguish than she ever had. First her father; now Thor. It was a day unlike any she had ever had. She could not even describe the unfathomable grief that tore her part at the thought of her father being dead. Dead by some assassin's hand, taken away from her without even a moment's notice. It just wasn't fair. He was the light of her life, and some stranger had taken him away from her for good.

When Gwen had discovered the news, she had wanted to die herself. Last night had been like one long nightmare, and this morning, like the peak of it. As his body went into the earth, she had wanted to leap in with him, and never come out.

When Gwen burst from the crowd, she had even been thinking about jumping over the edge of the cliff herself. Until Thor arrived.

Seeing him, in some strange way, snapped her out of it, had made things better, had taken her mind off her father—although in another way, it had also made things far worse. She was still furious with him, still burned with anger for his making a fool of her in that brothel. She had taken a chance by being with a commoner, and he had proved everyone right about her recklessness. Including her mother. She felt shamed beyond what she could imagine.

And now the gall of him, to show up here, to try to make things right, while he himself admitted that he had been there, with that woman. The thought of it was enough to make her sick.

As she watched Thor hurry off, down the trail, away from the cliff, Krohn beside him, despite herself she felt a sense of longing, of despair; she wondered how things could get any worse. She looked out over the endless expanse, over the dips and valleys of the Kolvian Cliffs, looking westward over the kingdom. She knew that somewhere, farther than she could see, lay the Highlands, and beyond that the McCloud's kingdom. She wondered if her sister was already over there, with her new husband, if she were enjoying her life. She was lucky to be far from here.

But then again, her sister had never been that close with their father, and she wondered if she would even care if she heard news of his demise. She, Gwen, of all of them, had been the closest to him. Reese and Kendrick had been close, too, and she could see how hard it hit them. Godfrey had hated their father, though now, looking at him, she was surprised to see his upset, too. And then there was Gareth. He still looked as cold and emotionless as ever, even with their father's death. He had looked preoccupied. As if his eyes were already on the power he so desperately wanted to seize.

The thought of it made her shudder. She remembered her father's fateful speech, his assigning the rule of the kingdom to her for some far-off day, for a day she was sure she would never see. She remembered her vow to him, her promise that she would rule. And now, here she was, the kingdom plopped into her hand. Would they make her rule? She hoped not. How could she? And yet, she had vowed to her father that she would. What was to become of her?

"There you are," came a voice.

Gwen turned to see Reese, standing a few feet away, looking at her with concern.

"I was worried for you."

"What did you think, I was going to jump?" she snapped back at him, too harsh. She didn't mean for it to come out that way, but she was reeling, barely able to control herself.

"No, of course not," Reese said. "I was just worried about you, that's all."

"Don't worry about me," she said. "I am your older sister. I can take care of myself."

"I never said you couldn't," Reese said, defensive. "I just want you know…you're not the only one who's suffering. I loved father, too."

Gwen thought about that. She saw the tears in his eyes and knew that he was right; she was being selfish. Their father's death was hurting them all.

"I am sorry," she said softly. "I know you did. And I know he loved you, too. Very much. In fact, I think he saw himself most in you."

Reese looked up at her with a hopeful, sad look. He looked so lost, her heart broke for him. Who would raise him now? she wondered. He was fourteen, not a boy, but hardly a man. This was the time a boy needed his father the most, needed a man to model after. Since the news of his death, her mother had been nearly catatonic, withdrawn, not present for any of them. Her older sister was gone; Gareth was never present; Godfrey lived in the alehouse; and Kendrick lived on the battlefield. Gwen felt that it fell on her to be Reese's mother and father.

"You are going to be fine," she said, gaining courage herself as she said it. "We are all going to be fine."

"Did I see Thor come this way?" Reese asked.

The thought of it made Gwen's stomach turn.

"He did," she answered flatly. "And I sent him on his way."

"What do you mean?" Recessed asked warily. "I thought you two were close."

She grunted.

"Not anymore. Not after what he did."

"What did he do?" he asked, wide-eyed.

"As if to tell me you don't know? As if to tell me the whole kingdom does not know what a fool he has made of me?"

"A fool? What are you talking about?" Reese asked, sounding genuinely curious.

She studied him and could see he genuinely did not seem to know, which surprised her. She had imagined that the whole kingdom knew, and was making fun of her behind her back. Maybe it was not as bad as she had imagined; maybe it was not as bad as Alton had said.

"I heard all about his exploits at the brothel. His time with those women," she said.

Reese's face dropped.

"And who did you hear this from?"

Gwen paused, suddenly not so sure of herself.

"Why, Alton, of course."

Reese grinned.

"And you believed it?"

Gwen stared back, feeling a flutter in her chest, beginning to wonder if she had made some sort of awful mistake.

"What do you mean?" she asked.

"I was there with him that day," Reese said. "In the brothel. We all were. The entire Legion. After the hunt. He did nothing wrong. It was more tavern than brothel. In fact, I was by his side when the women came out. He had been surprised to discover there were any women there at all. He had, in fact, tried to flee. The men shoved him forward. He did not go forward willingly."

"But still, he went forward," Gwen said accusingly.

Reese shook his head adamantly.

"You have been misinformed. Thor did nothing. He reached the landing and passed out. He hit the floor before a woman could lay a hand on him. He did not touch any woman, I assure you. Alton was lying to you. It was Alton that made a fool of you. Your pride remains intact."

Gwen felt her whole body flush at his words. She felt overwhelmed with relief, but also with shame. She had been wrong about Thor. She thought of her harsh words to him. She had never meant to call him a commoner; she had not known why she'd said that. She sounded so haughty, so arrogant; she was disgusted with herself. How could she have been so cruel?

"What did you say to him exactly?" Reese asked.

Gwen lowered her chin.

"Something stupid. Very, very stupid. Something I did not mean."

Gwen felt overwhelmed; she reached in and gave Reese a hug, and he hugged her back. She cried over his shoulder.

"I miss our father," she said.

"I know," Reese said over her shoulder, his words muffled. "I miss him, too."

Reese pulled back and looked at her.

"I will talk to Thor. Whatever you said, I will try to smooth it over."

Gwen slowly shook her head, unsure.

"Some things cannot be taken back," she said softly.

CHAPTER EIGHT

Gareth walked with his brothers, Kendrick, Godfrey and Reese, and with his sister, Gwen, into the huge castle hall, packed with hundreds of the king's men, who milled about in an agitated way. The small group of them were ushered through the crowd, as knights from all provinces of the Ring reached out to offer condolences as they went.

"We loved your father, sire," said a knight to Gareth, a burly man he had never met. "He was a great king."

Gareth did not know these men—and he did not care to know them. He did not want their sympathy. It was a sympathy he did not share. Now that he had time to reflect on it, to let the reality of it sink in, he was glad his father was dead. His father had never held any love for him, and while the night before Gareth had initially been torn over it, he was beginning to feel differently about the matter. He now felt a great sense of relief—even victorious—that his assassination plot had succeeded. Although he had not actually killed him himself, and although he had not even died in the way he had planned, at least he had set the plan into motion. Without him, none of this would have ever happened.

Gareth looked around at these knights, at this great crowd, so chaotic, and was shocked to realize that he was responsible for all this. He had single-handedly changed the lives of all of these men, whether they knew it or not.

The group of siblings was ushered through the crowd by several attendants, as they headed for the distant hall, where the king's council was waiting to meet with them all. Gareth felt a knot in his chest as they marched forward, wondering what lay in store for them. Of course, they had to name a successor. They could not leave the kingdom to go on without one, like a ship without a rudder. Gareth hoped that they would name him. Who else could they name?

Maybe they would use the meeting to name his sister as ruler. He looked at his siblings all around him, their faces set, grim and silent, and wondered if they would fight for the throne. They probably would; they all hated him, and after all, their father had made it clear that he wanted Gwen to rule. This was the one moment in his life that he really needed to fight. If he walked out of this meeting successful, he would walk out as ruler of the kingdom.

Yet he also wondered, with a sinking feeling, if maybe he was walking into a setup. Maybe they were summoning him to accuse him, in front of everyone, to present evidence that he had killed his father; maybe they would drag him off to be executed. His emotions swayed from optimism to anxiety, as he marveled at what drastic outcomes the meeting could have.

Finally they made it through the crowd, who were clearly waiting to hear the rulings of the council, and were ushered through an open arched door, promptly closed behind them by four guards.

Spread out before them was the grand, semi-circular table of the council, behind which sat the advisers to the king—in the same place they had sat for hundreds of years. It was strange to walk in here and not see his father seated on that throne. The huge, carved throne sat empty, for the first time in his life. The councilmembers faced it, as if waiting for a ruler to drop down from the sky and lead them.

The group of them walked down the center of the room, Gareth's heart thumping, between the two halves of the semi-circular table, and found themselves, as they turned, standing before the dozen councilmembers. They all stared back, grim, and Gareth could not help but wonder if this were an inquisition. Seated with them, in a dainty throne off to the side, flanked by her attendants, was his mother. She watched over the proceedings with a blank face, and looked frozen in shock.

Seated at the center of the table was Aberthol, the oldest of the bunch, a scholar and historian, mentor of kings for three generations, looking positively ancient, etched with wrinkles, wearing his long, regal purple robe which he had probably worn since the days when his father was a boy. Being the eldest, and the wisest, the other council members clearly looked to him to lead the proceedings. He was flanked by Brom, Kolk, Owen, the treasurer, Bradaigh, his adviser on external affairs; Earnan, his tax collector; Duwayne, his adviser on the masses; and Kelvin, the representative of the nobles. It was a formidable group of men, and Gareth examined them all, trying to see if any were preparing to condemn him. None seemed to stare at him directly.

Aberthol cleared his throat as he looked down at a scroll, then looked up silently at the group of siblings.

"Our council wishes to begin by extending our sincerest condolences for the death of your father. He was a great man, and a great king. His presence in this chamber, and in this kingdom, will be sorely missed. I think it's fair to say that this kingdom will never be the same without him. I had known him since the time he could walk, I counseled his father before him, and he was a dear friend to me. We will do everything in our power to find his assassin."

Aberthol slowly surveyed them, and Gareth tried not to be paranoid as he saw him looking at him.

"I have known the lot of you since you were born; I am certain that your father is very proud of you. As much as we would like to give you time to mourn, there are pressing matters of ruling this kingdom that must be addressed. Which is why we have summoned you here today."

He cleared his throat.

"The most pressing matter is our inquiry into your father's assassination. We will gather a commission to investigate the cause and manner of his death, and to bring the killer to justice. Until we do, I think it is safe to say that no member of this kingdom will sit at ease. Including myself."

Gareth could have sworn he saw his eyes stop at him, and he wondered if he were giving him a message. He looked away, trying not to let his mind go there. Gareth's mind raced, as he scrambled to come up with a plan to divert attention away from him. He needed to frame a killer, and he needed to do it quickly.

"In the meantime, we sit in a kingdom without a king. It is a restless empire, and this is not a safe place to be. The longer we lack a ruler, the longer others may conspire to seize power, to overthrow the royal court. I needn't tell you that there are many men that would like to have the throne."

He sighed.

"The law of the Ring holds that the kingship must pass to the firstborn son of the father. In this case, it pains me to add, the firstborn *legitimate* son—with no offense meant to you, Kendrick."

Kendrick bowed his head.

"None taken, sire."

"That would mean then," Aberthol said, clearing his throat, "that the kingship must pass to Gareth."

Gareth felt a thrill at his words. He felt a rush of power beyond what he could describe.

"But my Liege, what of our sister, Gwendolyn?" Kendrick shot back.

"Gwendolyn?" Aberthol asked, surprise in his voice.

"Before our father died," Kendrick continued, "he told us it was his wish that Gwendolyn should succeed him."

Gareth's face burned red, as the entire council turned and stared at Gwendolyn. She looked down to the ground, distraught, maybe even embarrassed. He assumed she was just putting on a show of humility. She probably wanted to rule even more than he.

"Is this true, Gwendolyn?" Aberthol asked.

"It is, my lord," she answered softly, still looking down. "It is what my father wished. He made me vow to him that I would accept. And I vowed. I wish I hadn't. I can think of nothing I want less."

An excited and disturbed gasp spread amongst the council members, as they turned to each other, clearly caught off guard.

"A woman has never ruled the kingdom," Brom said, agitated.

"Much less a young girl," Kolk added.

"If we were to hand over the kingship to a girl," Kelvin said, "surely the nobles would rebel, would vie for power. It would put us in a position of weakness."

"Not to mention the McClouds," Bradaigh added. "They would attack. They would test us."

Aberthol raised a hand, and slowly, they all quieted. He sat there, looking down at the table, lowering his hand, his palm flat on it, and looked like an ancient tree, rooted to the place.

"Whether the king wished for it or not, it is not for us to say. That is not the issue here. The law is the issue. And legally speaking, our late king's most unusual choice of an heir was never ratified. And without ratification, it is not law."

"But it would have been ratified at the next council meeting!" Kendrick said.

"Perhaps," Aberthol responded, "but to his bad fortune, that meeting had not yet come. Thus, we have no written record, and no ratification into law."

"But we have witnesses!" Kendrick yelled out, impassioned.

"It is true!" Reese yelled out. "I was there!"

"As was I!" Godfrey yelled.

Gareth held his tongue, even as the others looked at him. Inside, he was burning with rage. He felt as if his dreams of being king were crumbling all around him. He despised his siblings more than ever, who all seemed to gang up on him.

"I'm afraid that witnesses alone do not suffice when it comes to a matter as important as the kingship," Aberthol said. "All official decrees must be ratified by the council. Without this, they cannot become law. Which means the law must stand as it always has, for centuries of MacGil kings: the eldest, the firstborn, must inherit. I am sorry, Gwendolyn."

"Mother!" Kendrick yelled, pleading, turning towards the Queen. "You know father's wishes! Do something! Tell them!"

But the queen sat there, hands folded in her lap, staring into space. She was in a catatonic state, and she was inscrutable.

After several moments of silence, Kendrick finally turned back to the council.

"But it is not right!" he yelled. "Whether ratified or not, it was the king's will. Our father's will. You all served him. You should respect that. Gareth should not rule. Gwendolyn should."

"My dear brother, please, it is OK," Gwen said softly to Kendrick, laying a hand on his wrist.

"And who is to say that *I* should not rule?" Gareth finally yelled back, seething, unable to take it anymore. "I am the king's firstborn son, after all. Unlike you," he spat to Kendrick.

Gareth's face burned with anger, and he immediately regretted it. He knew he should have kept his mouth shut, should have waited and let it seem as if the kingship fell to him unwanted. But he was unable to contain himself. He could tell by the look in Kendrick's eyes that he'd hurt him with his words. He was glad that he did.

"Suffice all of this say," Aberthol said slowly, "that the law is the law. I am sorry. But Gareth, son of King MacGil, in accordance with the ancient law of the Ring, I hereby proclaim you to be the eighth MacGil king of the Western Kingdom of the Ring. Hear ye all here assembled: do you hear our proclamation?"

"Hear ye!" came the response.

An iron staff was slammed, and a metallic ring boomed through the room.

Gareth flinched, feeling his whole body shake. With that boom, he felt himself transported.

With that sound, he was King.

He could not believe it.

He was King.

CHAPTER NINE

King McCloud rode at the head of the small military contingent, dressed in his battle gear, wearing the distinctive burnt-orange armor of the McClouds. A tall, stout man, twice as wide as any other, there was little fat on him; with a short, cropped red beard, long hair mostly gray, a wide nose, crushed in from too many battles, and an even wider jaw, he was a man who feared nothing in life. He was already, having just reached his fiftieth year, famed as the most aggressive and brutal McCloud that had lived. It was a reputation he cherished.

McCloud was a man who had always squeezed from life whatever it could give him. And what it would not give him, he would take. In fact, he liked to take, more than to receive; he enjoyed making others miserable, and enjoyed ruling his kingdom with an iron fist. He enjoyed showing no mercy, keeping his soldiers in line with a discipline unlike any McCloud had ever wielded. And it worked. His dozen men rode behind him now in perfect order, and none would ever dare speak back to him, or do the smallest thing against his will. That included his son, the prince, who rode close behind him, and a dozen of his best archers, who rode behind his son.

McCloud and his men had been riding hard all day. They had breached the Eastern Crossing of the Canyon early in the morning, and his small armed contingent had continued east, charging without a break through the dusty plains of the Nevari, on guard for an ambush. They rode and rode, as the second sun rose and slipped. Now, finally, covered in dust from the plains, McCloud spotted the Ambrek Sea on the horizon.

The galloping of horses filled his ears and now, the smell of the ocean air reached him. It was a cool summer afternoon, the second sun long in the sky, casting shades of turquoise and pink on the horizon. McCloud felt his hair being blown back in the wind, and looked forward to arriving on the shore. It had been years since he had seen the ocean: it was too risky to venture here lightly given that they had to breach the Canyon and then ride fifty miles in unprotected territory. Of course, the McClouds had their own fleet of ships in the waters, as the MacGils had on their side of the Ring—but still, it was always a risky business, being beyond the energy shield of the Canyon. Every now and again the Empire took out one of their ships, and there was little the McClouds could do about it. The Empire vastly outnumbered them.

But this time, it was different. A McCloud ship had been intercepted at sea by the Empire, and usually, the Empire took the McClouds for ransom. McCloud had never paid a single ransom, something he was proud of; instead, he always let the Empire kill his men. He refused to embolden them.

But something had shifted, because this time they had freed his men and sent the ship back with a message: they wanted to meet with McCloud. McCloud assumed it could be only about one thing: breaching the Canyon. Invading the Ring. And partnering with them to take down the MacGils. For years, the Empire had been trying to convince the McClouds to allow them to breach the Canyon, the energy shield, to let them inside the Ring so that they could conquer and dominate the last remaining territory on the planet. In returned, they promised a sharing of power.

The question burning in McCloud's mind was this: what was in it for him? How much would the Empire be willing to give him? For years, he had turned down their overtures. But now, things were different. The MacGils had grown too strong, and McCloud was beginning to realize that he might not ever achieve his dream of controlling the Ring without foreign help.

As they neared the beach, McCloud glanced over his shoulder at his son's new bride, riding with him, his trophy wife from the MacGils. How stupid MacGil had been to give his daughter away. Had he really thought this would cause peace between them? Did he think McCloud was that soft, that dumb? Of course, McCloud had accepted the bride, just as he would accept a herd of cattle. It was always good to have possessions, to have bargaining chips. But that didn't make him ready for peace. If anything, it emboldened him. It made him want to take over the MacGil side of the Ring even more, especially after that wedding, after entering King's

Court and seeing their bounty. McCloud wanted it all for himself. He *burned* to have it all for himself.

They rode onto the sand, the horses' hooves sinking, his weight shifting, as the group of them neared the water's edge. The cool mist struck McCloud in the face, and it felt good to be back here, on this shore he hadn't seen for years. Life had made him too busy as a King; it was on days like this that he resolved to give up all of his duties, to spend more time living again.

Above the waves, in the distance, he could already see the caravan of black Empire ships: they sailed with a yellow flag, with an emblem of a black shield in its center, two horns protruding from it. The closest was hardly a hundred yards from shore, anchored, clearly awaiting their arrival. Behind it sat two dozen more. McCloud wondered; was this just a show of strength? Or was the Empire going to ambush them? This was the chance he took. McCloud hoped it was the former. After all, killing him would do no good: it would not help them breach the Canyon, which was what they really wanted. This was why McCloud only brought a dozen men with him: he figured it would make him seem stronger. Though he did bring a dozen of his best archers, all with poisoned arrows at the ready, in case something should happen.

McCloud stopped at the water's edge and his men stopped around him, their horses breathing hard. He dismounted and the others followed, huddled close around him. The Empire must have spotted them, because McCloud saw a small wooden boat lowered down its side, towards the water, inside it at least a dozen of those savages. They were preparing to come ashore. McCloud looked at those sails and felt his stomach turn: he hated dealing with these savages, these creatures who he knew would gladly betray him, would gladly breach the Canyon and override both sides of the Ring if they could.

McCloud's men gathered close around him.

"At any sign of trouble, light your arrows and let them fly. Aim for their sails. You can set the whole fleet on fire with a dozen arrows each."

"Yes, sire," came the chorus of voices.

His son, Devon, stood at his side, while his newfound wife, the MacGil woman, next to him, looking nervously at the water. It had been McCloud's idea to bring the woman here. He wanted to instill fear in her. He wanted her to know that she was McCloud property now, that she relied on them and them solely for her safety. He wanted her to learn that her father and his kingdom were far behind, and that she would never return.

It was working. She stood there, terrified, practically clinging to Devon's side. Devon, the stupid son that he was, reveled in it. He didn't realize the value in any of this. To McCloud's disgust, it even looked like he was smitten by the girl.

"What do you think they want from us?" Devon asked him, coming up close.

"What else could they want?" McCloud snapped. "Stupid boy. To open the gates to the Canyon."

"Will you let them? Will you make a deal with them, father?"

McCloud turned and glared at his boy, sending his wrath through his eyes, until finally his boy looked away.

"I never discuss my thoughts with anyone. You will know my decision when I make it. In the meantime, stand and watch. And learn."

They all stood there in the thick silence as the Empire boat neared shore. It was still several minutes away, rowing hard against the waves, which crashed outward, towards the sea, in these strange currents of the Ambrek. They broke about a hundred yards out, and one had to fight them, to get over them, to make it to shore. It made McCloud happy he was not rowing: he remembered from his youth what hard work it was, as he watched the boat crest and crash in wave after wave.

Suddenly, McCloud heard the galloping of a horse. It made no sense: there was supposed to be no one within miles of him, and he was immediately on guard. His men spun, too, and they all drew their swords and bows, as they prepared for an attack. McCloud had feared this: had it all just been a trap?

But as he watched the horizon, he did not see an army approach; he was confused by what he saw. It was a single horse, galloping over the plains, raising a cloud of dust, and continuing to ride right onto the beach, right for them. The man who rode was one of his: dressed in orange, with the blue stripes of a messenger across his shoulders.

A messenger, racing towards them, in this barren place. He must have followed them all the way from the kingdom. McCloud wondered: what could be so urgent that his people would send him a messenger here, in this place? It must be significant news.

The messenger rode right up to them and dismounted from his horse while it had barely stopped. He stood there, reeling hard, gasping for air, took several steps toward McCloud, and kneeled down before him, bowing his head

"My liege, I bring you news from the kingdom," he said, gasping.

"What is it, then?" McCloud snapped, impatient, checking back over his shoulder at the Empire ship, rowing its way closer. Why, now, of all moments, had this messenger had to come? At the moment when he most needed to stand on guard against the Empire?

"Quickly, out with it!" McCloud yelled.

The messenger stood, breathing hard.

"My liege, the MacGil king is dead."

A surprised gasp erupted from his men—most of all, from McCloud himself.

"Dead?" he asked, uncomprehending. He had just left him, a king at the height of his power.

"Murdered," the messenger replied. "Stabbed to death in his chamber."

A horrible shriek arose beside him, and McCloud turned to see the MacGil daughter, wailing, flailing her arms hysterically.

"NO!" she screamed. "My father!"

She was shrieking and flailing, and Devon tried to stop her, to grab her arms, but she could not be pacified.

"Let me go!" she cried. "I must go back. Right now! I must see him!"

"He's dead," Devon said to her.

"NO!" she wailed.

McCloud could not afford to have the Empire see one of their women screaming, out of control. Nor did he want her to give away the news. He had to quiet her.

McCloud stepped forward and punched the woman across the face, so hard, he knocked her out. She collapsed into Devon's arms—and he looked up at his father, horrified.

"What have you done?" Devon called out. "She is my bride!" he snapped, indignant.

"She is my property," McCloud corrected. He glared at his son long enough, until his son looked away.

McCloud turned back to the messenger.

"Are you certain he's dead?"

"Quite certain, sire. Their entire side of the Ring mourns. His funeral was this morning. He is dead.

"What's more," the messenger added, "they have already named a new king. His firstborn son. Gareth."

Gareth, McCloud thought. How perfect. The weakest of the lot, the one who would make the worst king. McCloud could not have asked for better news.

McCloud nodded slowly, rubbing his beard, taking it all in. This was opportune news, indeed. MacGil, his rival, dead, after all these decades. He could hardly believe it. Assassinated. He wondered by whom. He would like to thank the man. He was only sorry he had not thought of it himself. He of course had tried to send assassins over the years, had tried to infiltrate the court, but had never been successful. And now, one of MacGil's own men had succeeded where he could not.

This changed everything.

McCloud turned back, took several steps towards the sea, and watched the Empire boat get closer and closer. It crested the waves, and was now hardly thirty yards from shore. MacGil stepped towards the water and stood there alone, several feet away from the others, hands on his hips, thinking. This news would change his meeting with the Empire. With MacGil dead, and with that weakling as king, the MacGils would be vulnerable. Now, indeed, would be the perfect time to attack. Now they might not even need the help of the empire.

The boat came to shore, and McCloud stepped back as it reached the sand, his men flanking him. There were at least a dozen Empire men inside, rowing hard, all savages, all dressed in the bright red loincloths of the Wilds. As they all stood, he saw how huge and imposing they were. McCloud was a huge man himself—but even so, each of these savages was at least a head taller than he, with broad shoulders, muscles rippling on their red skin. They had huge jaws, like an animal, their eyes sat too far apart, and their noses were sunken into their skin in a small triangle. With narrow lips, long fangs, and curled yellow horns coming from their bald heads, McCloud had to admit to himself that he felt afraid. These were monsters.

Their leader, Andronicus, stood at the rear of the boat, and he was even taller than the others. He was a specimen. Nearly twice as tall as McCloud, his yellow eyes flashed as he smiled an evil smile, showing rows of sharp teeth. In two strides, he jumped from the boat, and stood there on the shore. He wore a shining necklace, its rope of gold, and on it hanging the shrunken heads of his enemies. He reached up and fingered it, and his hands, like the others, ended in three sharp claws.

As he jumped onto the sand, his men jumped out around him, forming a semi-circle with their leader in the middle.

Andronicus. McCloud had heard stories of this man. He had heard of his cruelty, his barbarism, his iron control over the entire Empire, every single province except the Ring. McCloud had never fully believed the stories of how imposing he was, not until now, as he stood before him. He felt it himself. For the first time in as long as he could remember, he felt in danger, even with his men around him. He regretted calling this meeting.

Andronicus stepped forward and brought his arms out wide to his sides, palms up, claws glistening, and smiled a wide smile, more of a snarl, a gurgling sound like a snarl coming from the back of his throat

"Greetings," he said, his voice impossibly deep. "We send you a gift from the Wilds."

He nodded, and one of his men stepped forward and held out a large, bejeweled chest. It sparkled in the late afternoon sun, and McCloud looked down at it and wondered.

The attendant pulled back the lid and reached in, and held out the severed head of a man. McCloud was horrified as he looked down at it: the man looked to be in his fifties, eyes wide open in a death stare, with a bushy black beard, blood still dripping from what was left of his throat. McCloud stared at it, and wondered. He looked up at Andronicus and tried to seem unaffected.

"Is it a gift?" McCloud demanded. "Or a threat?"

Andronicus smiled.

"Both," he answered. "In our kingdom, it is a ritual to give as a gift the severed head of one of your enemies. It is said that if you drink the blood from the throat, while it is still fresh, it will give you the power of many men."

The attendant reached out and McCloud grabbed the bloody, matted hair of the skull, and held it out. The look of it disgusted him, but he did not want to tip his hand to these savages. He calmly reached back and handed it to one of his people, without looking at it again.

"Thank you," he said.

Andronicus smiled wider, and McCloud had the uncanny feeling that he was seeing right through him. He felt off guard.

"Do you know why we have called this meeting?" Andronicus asked.

"I can guess," McCloud answered. "You need our help to access the Ring. To cross the Canyon."

Andronicus nodded, his eyes twinkling with something like excitement and lust.

"We want this very badly. And we know that you can provide this for us."

"Why don't you go to the MacGils?" McCloud asked the question that had been burning on his mind. "Why choose us?"

"They are closed-minded. Unlike you."

"But why do you think we are different?" McCloud asked, testing him, wanting to know how much he knew.

"My spies tell us that you and the MacGils do not get along. You want control of the Ring. But you know by now that you will never have it. If this is truly what you want, then you need a powerful ally to help you gain it. You will let us into the Ring. And we will help you gain the other half of the kingdom."

McCloud studied him, wondering. Andronicus' eyes were inscrutable, large and yellow and flashing; he had no idea what he was thinking.

"And what's in it for you?" McCloud asked.

Andronicus smiled.

"Of course, once our army helps you overtake the Ring, then the Ring will be part of the Empire. You will be one of our sovereign territories. You will have to answer to me, but you will be free to run it as you wish. I will allow you to rule all of the Ring. You will keep all the spoils for yourself. We both win."

McCloud studied him, rubbing his beard.

"But if I gain all the spoils and can rule it as I wish, what do you gain?"

Andronicus smiled.

"The Ring is the only kingdom on this planet that I do not control. And I do not like things that I cannot control." Suddenly, his smiled turned into a grimace, and McCloud had a glimpse of his fierceness. "It sets a bad example for the other kingdoms."

As the waves crashed all around them and the sun dipped lower, McCloud stood there, thinking. It was the answer he had expected. But he still didn't have the answer to the question burning most in his mind.

"And how do I know I can trust you?" McCloud asked.

Andronicus smiled wide.

"You don't," he answered.

The honesty of his answer surprised McCloud, and, ironically, made him trust him even more.

"But we, too, don't know if we can trust you," he added. "After all, our armies will be vulnerable inside the Ring. You could seal off the Canyon once we were inside. You could ambush our men. We must trust each other."

"But you have far more men than we do," McCloud answered.

"But every life is precious," Andronicus said.

Now McCloud knew that he was lying. Did he really expect him to believe that? Andronicus had millions of soldiers at his disposal, and McCloud had heard stories of his sacrificing entire armies, millions of men, to gain a small piece of ground, just to make a point. Would he do the same to betray McCloud? Would he let McCloud control the Ring, and then, one day, when he wasn't expecting it, kill him, too?

McCloud thought it over. Before today, it had been a chance he'd be willing to take: after all, it would enable him to control the entire Ring, to oust the MacGils, and the way McCloud saw it, he could betray the Empire first, use their men to conquer the Ring, then re-activate the shield, and kill the Empire men stuck inside.

But after today, after hearing that MacGil was dead, that Gareth was the new king, McCloud felt differently. He might not need the Empire after all. If only he had received this message sooner, before he'd agreed to this meeting. But McCloud didn't want to completely alienate the Empire either; they might come in useful, at some later date. He had to stall them, to buy time while he tried his new strategy.

He reached up and stroked his beard, pretending to consider the offer, as the waves crashed all around him and the sky turned purple.

"I am grateful for your offer, and I will consider it thoroughly."

Andronicus suddenly stepped forward, so close that McCloud could smell his awful breath, as he scowled down. He wondered if he had offended him, and had an impulse to reach down for his sword. But he was too nervous to do so. He felt this man could tear him in two if he chose.

"Don't think too long," he seethed, all his humor gone. "I don't like a man who needs time to think. And my offer will not stand long. If you do not let us in, we will find a way in. And if we find a way in our own, we will crush you. Keep that in mind as you consider the possibilities."

McCloud glowered, reddening. No one ever spoke to him this way.

"Is that a threat?" McCloud asked. He wanted to sound confident, but despite himself, he found his voice shaking.

A deep, throaty sound rippled through Andronicus' chest, then up through his throat. At first McCloud thought it was a cough—but then he realized it was a laugh.

"I never threaten," he said down to McCloud. "You will come to learn that about me very, very well."

CHAPTER TEN

Thor walked with his head down, downcast, kicking pebbles on the road. Krohn walked at his side and Ephistopheles circled somewhere high above, as he made his way slowly to the Legion barracks. Since the funeral, his encounter with Gwen, he felt deflated. The pain of watching MacGil being lowered into the earth took something out of him—as if a part of him sank into the earth with him. The king had taken him under his wing, had shown him kindness, had given him Ephistopheles, had been the only father figure he'd ever had. He felt as if he owed him something, that it had been his responsibility to save him, and somehow, he had failed. As the bells had tolled, Thor felt as if they tolled the announcement of his failure.

Then there was his encounter with Gwen. She hated him now, that much was obvious. Nothing he could say would change her mind. Even worse, her true thoughts came out today: she felt he was beneath her. A commoner. It seemed Alton had been right all the while. The thought of it crushed him. First he had lost the king; then he had lost the girl he had grown to love.

As he walked back towards the Legion, he realized it was the one thing left that he could cling to here. He cared not for his village, or his father, or his brothers. Without the Legion and Reese—and Krohn—he did not know what he would have left.

Krohn yelped and Thor looked up and saw the barracks before him. The king's banner flew at half mast, and he could already see dozens of boys sulking, and could tell the mood was somber. It was a day of mourning here. The king, their leader, had been murdered, and worse, no one knew who did it, or why. There also seemed to be an air of expectancy. Would the armies be disbanded? The Legion with it?

Thor saw the wary looks of the boys as he walked through the large, arched stone gate. They were stopping and staring at him. He wondered what they thought of him. Just the night before he'd been thrown into the dungeon, and Thor was sure that the rumor had spread that he had something to do with poisoning the king. Did these boys know that he was vindicated? Did they still suspect him? Or did they think he was a hero for trying to save him?

From their looks, he could not tell. But he did know that the tension in the air was thick, and he could tell that he clearly had been a subject of conversation.

As Thor entered the large wooden structure of the barracks, he noticed dozens of boys stuffing their clothes and various objects into canvas sacks. It looked, oddly, as if the Legion were packing up. Was it disbanding? he wondered, in a sudden panic.

"There you are," came a voice he recognized.

He turned to see O'Connor standing there, smiling in his typical good-natured way, his bright red hair and freckles framing his face. He reached out and clasped Thor's forearm.

"I feel like I haven't seen you in days. Are you okay? I heard you were thrown in the clink. What happened?"

"Hey look, it's Thor!" yelled a voice.

Thor turned to see Elden hurrying towards him, a good-natured smile on his face, embracing him. Thor was still amazed at Elden's attitude towards him, ever since he had saved his life across the Canyon, especially when he recalled the hostile greeting Elden had once given him.

Coming up beside him were the twins, Conval and Conven.

"Glad to have you back," Conven said, embracing Thor in a hug.

"And I," Conval echoed.

Thor was relieved to see them all, especially as he realized that they did not assume he had anything to do with the murder.

"It's true," Thor responded, looking at O'Connor, not sure which question to answer first. "I was thrown into the dungeon. At first they thought I had something to do with the king's poisoning. But after he was killed, they realized I had nothing to do with it."

"So they let you free?" O'Connor asked.

Thor thought about that, not quite sure how to respond.

"Not exactly. I escaped."

They all looked at him, wide-eyed.

"Escaped?" Elden asked.

"Once I was out, Reese helped me. He brought me to the king."

"You saw the king before he died?" Conval asked, shocked.

Thor nodded back.

"He knows I am innocent."

"What else did he say?" O'Connor asked.

Thor hesitated. He felt funny telling them about what the king said about his destiny, about being special. He didn't want to seem like he was boasting, or seem delusional, or cause envy. So he decided to omit that part and just tell them how it ended.

Thor looked him in the eye. "He said: avenge me."

The others looked at the floor, grim.

"Do you have any idea who did it?" O'Connor asked.

Thor shook his head.

"As much as you do."

"I would love to catch him," Conven said.

"As would I," Elden added.

"But I don't understand," Thor said, looking around, "what is all this packing? It seems as if everyone is getting to leave."

"We are," O'Connor said. "Including you."

O'Connor reached over, grabbed a canvas sack, and threw it at Thor. It hit Thor hard in the chest, and he grabbed it before it hit the ground.

"What do you mean?" Thor asked, puzzled.

"The Hundred starts tomorrow," Elden answered. "We are all preparing."

"The Hundred?" Thor asked.

"Do you know nothing?" Conval asked.

"It seems we have to teach this young one everything," Conven added.

Conven stepped forward and draped an arm across Thor's shoulder.

"Don't worry, my friend. There's always much to learn in the Legion. The Hundred is the Legion's way of making us all hardened warriors—and weeding us out. It is a rite of passage. Every year, at summertime, they send us for a hundred days of the most grueling training you'll ever know. Some of us will return. Those who do are granted honors, weapons, and a permanent place in the Legion."

Thor looked around, still puzzled. "But why are you packing?"

"Because the Hundred is not here," Elden explained. "They ship us off. Literally. Far from here. We must journey across the Canyon, into the Wilds, across the Tartuvian Sea, and all the way to the Isle of Mist. It is a hundred days of hell. We all dread it. But we must go through it, if we are to stay in the Legion. Our ship sails tomorrow, so pack quickly."

Thor looked down at the sack in his hand, unbelieving. He could hardly imagine packing up what few things he had, crossing the Canyon into the Wilds, boarding a ship, and spending a hundred days on an island with all the Legion members. The thought of it excited him; it also terrified him. He'd never been on a ship, had never been across the sea. He loved the idea of advancing his skills, and he hoped he would make it and not be weeded out.

"Before you pack, you should report to your knight," Conven said. "You are squire to Kendrick now that Erec is gone, aren't you?"

Thor nodded back. "Yes, is he here?"

"He was outside with some of the other Knights," he answered. "He was preparing his horse, and I know he was looking for you."

As Thor stood there, his mind reeling, the thought of the Hundred excited him more than he could say. He wanted to be tested, to be pushed to the extreme, to see if he was as good as the others. And if he made it back—and he felt sure he would—he would return a stronger warrior.

"Are you sure that I'm included, that I'm allowed to come, too?" Thor asked.

"Of course you are," O'Connor said. "Assuming, of course, your knight doesn't need you here. You need his permission."

"Ask him," Elden said, "and be quick of it. There is much to do to prepare, and you're already far behind. The ships will not wait. And whoever does not go, cannot stay in the Legion."

"Try the armory," O'Connor said. "I saw Kendrick there just an hour ago."

Thor needed no prodding. He turned and ran from the barracks, out the door and across the fields, heading for the armory, Krohn yelping and running at his heels.

In moments he reached it, breathing hard, and there was Kendrick. He stood there alone, inside the armory, looking up at a wall of halberds. He looked pensive, intense, lost in thought. Thor felt as if he had intruded on private time, and felt guilty for interrupting.

Kendrick turned, and his eyes were red from crying. Thor thought of his father's funeral, remembered Kendrick lowering him into the ground, and felt terrible.

"Forgive me, sire," Thor said, catching his breath. He could see Kendrick's grief and felt bad for intruding. "I'm sorry to have disturbed you. I will leave."

As Thor turned to leave, his voice rang out.

"No. Stay. I would like to speak with you."

Thor turned back and waited, quiet, feeling Kendrick's pain. Kendrick waited a long time in the silence, examining the weaponry.

"My father, he loved you very much," Kendrick said. "He barely knew you, but I could see his love for you. It was real."

"Thank you, sire. I loved your father, too."

"The people in this kingdom, and in the royal court, they have never considered me to be his true son. Just because I was the son of another mother."

Kendrick turned to Thor, a determination in his eyes.

"But I *am* his son. As much as any of the others. He was a father to me. My only father. My father by blood. Just because we don't share the same mother, that doesn't make me any less," Kendrick reflected, reaching out and feeling the tip of a blade mounted on the wall, his eyes misty.

"I didn't know him long," Thor said, "but from what I saw, I could see his love for you, and his approval for you. It seemed to me to be as real and as strong as it was for any of the others."

Kendrick nodded, and Thor could see the appreciation in his eyes.

"He was a good man. He could be a hard man, and a tough man. But he was a good man, always fair. Our kingdom will not be the same without him."

"I wish you could be king," Thor said. "You would be the best one to rule."

Kendrick looked at the blade.

"Our kingdom has its law. And I must abide by it. I feel no envy for my brother, Gareth. The law dictates that he should rule, and he will. I do feel upset for my sister, who was passed over. That was not my father's wish. But for myself, I feel no regret. I don't know if Gareth will be a good King. But that is the law, and the law is not always fair. It is uncompromising: that is its nature."

Kendrick turned to Thor and examined him.

"And why have you come here?" he asked.

"Since Erec has left, I am told that I have been assigned to be your squire now. It is a great honor, sire. I can think of no finer knight."

"Ah, Erec," Kendrick said, looking off, glassy-eyed. "The finest knight we have. He's off for his Selection year, is he? Yes, I am pleased to have you as my squire, though I'm sure it will not last long. He'll be back. He can never leave King's Court for long."

Kendrick's expression suddenly morphed to one of understanding.

"So then you are coming to me to ask for permission to leave for The Hundred, are you?" he asked.

"Yes, sire. If that is okay with you. If it is not, I understand, and I am here to serve your needs."

Kendrick shook his head.

"Every young Legion member must go through The Hundred. It is a rite of passage. Selfishly, I would like you here, but I will not hold you back. Go. You'll come back a stronger warrior and a far better squire."

Thor was overwhelmed with gratitude towards Kendrick. He was about to ask him more about what lay in store with The Hundred when suddenly, the door to the armory burst open.

Thor and Kendrick turned to see Alton standing there, dressed in his royal finest, flanked by two guards of the royal court.

"There he is!" Alton screamed, pointing a haughty finger at Thor. "He's the one who struck me at the feast last night! A commoner, can you imagine? He struck a member of the royal family. He has violated our law. Arrest him!"

The two guards began to walk towards Thor, when Kendrick stepped forward and extracted his sword from his scabbard. The sound of the metal resonated in the armory, and as Kendrick stood there, fierce, holding his sword drawn before him, the two guards stopped in their tracks.

"Come any closer and you will pay the price," Kendrick threatened.

Thor could hear in his voice something deep and dark, a tone he had never heard before; the guards must have sensed it, too, because they dared not move.

"*I* am a member of the royal family," Kendrick corrected. "An *immediate* member. You, Alton, are not. You are son to a third cousin to the king. You guards will answer to me before you do to this pretender. And Thor is my squire. He is not to be touched. Not now or ever."

"But he broke the law!" Alton whined, bunching his fists like a baby. "A commoner cannot strike royalty!"

Kendrick smiled.

"In this case, I am very glad he did. In fact if I were there, I would have struck you myself. Whatever it is that you did, I'm sure you deserved it—and a lot more."

Alton scowled, turning red.

"I suggest you guards leave now. Or if you prefer, come closer, and pay the price. I'm itching to use my sword, actually."

The two guards gave each other a wary look, them both turned, re-sheathed their swords, and strutted out the armory. Only Alton was left there, standing alone, watching in frustration as the guards left.

"I would suggest you follow them quickly, before I find a good use for this blade in my hands."

Kendrick took a step forward, and Alton suddenly turned and ran out the door.

Kendrick, smiling, re-sheathed his sword and turned to Thor.

Thor was overwhelmed with gratitude, and he felt indebted to Kendrick, once again.

"I don't know how to thank you," Thor said.

Kendrick took a step forward and laid a hand on his shoulder.

"You already have. Just seeing the look on that pip's face actually made my day."

Kendrick laughed and Thor laughed, too. Then Kendrick looked at him with all seriousness.

"My father did not take people under his wing lightly. He saw something great in you. I see it, too. You will make us proud. Go to The Hundred and excel. Go and become the warrior that I know you will be."

*

Thor walked in the summer fields outside the Legion's compound, Krohn beside him, late in the day, the second sun dropping, filling the sky with spectacular pinks and oranges and purples. Krohn whined in delight as Thor led him deeper and deeper into the fields, giving him a chance to run, to play, to chase animals and to catch his dinner. Krohn carried an Ursutuay in his mouth now, a strange creature about the size of a rabbit, with purple fur and three heads, which he had proudly caught but minutes before.

Krohn was getting bigger and bigger before his eyes, now nearly twice the size from when he'd found him, and he was getting more of a desire to run and move about. Krohn was also becoming more playful, and he demanded that Thor take him farther and farther, and run with him. If Thor didn't run with him as much as he wanted, Krohn would nip playfully at Thor's ankles, and not let him alone until Thor chased him. Then, Krohn would take off with a delighted squeal, until Thor got tired of chasing him.

As the day had grown long, Thor had wanted a break from the barracks, from all the frantic preparations. He was all packed now, as was everybody else, and it felt as if they were counting down the hours until they left the Ring. Thor didn't know exactly when they were leaving, but he was told it would be within the next day or two. The mood in the barracks was tense and edgy, filled with anxiety for the trip to come and mourning for the king. It was like a time of great change had swept through them suddenly.

Thor wanted one last chance to be alone before the trip, to clear his head, still swimming with the death of the king, and with his encounter with Gwendolyn. His mind drifted to thoughts of Erec, of where he must be now. Would he ever return? He thought of how temporary life could be: everything seemed so permanent, but it rarely was. It made him feel more alive, and less alive, at the same time.

"Nothing is as it seems," came a voice.

Thor wheeled, and was shocked to see Argon, standing there, dressed in his scarlet robe, holding a staff and looking out to the distant horizon, into the vast expanse of the open sky. Thor, as always, wondered how Argon had appeared here so suddenly. Thor looked at him, and felt both a sense of dread and excitement.

"I was searching for you, after the funeral," Thor said. "There are so many questions I have for you. Even before the death. But I could not find you."

"I do not always wish to be found," Argon said. His eyes were shining, a light blue.

Thor stared at him, wondering how much Argon was seeing right now. Did he see the future? Would he tell him if he did?

"We're leaving tomorrow," Thor said, "for The Hundred."

"I know," Argon answered.

"Will I return?" Thor asked, dying to know.

Argon looked away.

"Will I still be in the Legion? Will I pass the test? Become a great warrior?"

Argon stared back, expressionless.

"Many questions," he said, and turned and looked away. Thor realized he was not going to respond to any of them.

"If I told you your future, it might affect it," Argon added. "Every choice you make, that is what creates it."

"But I saw MacGil's future," Thor said. "In that dream. I saw that he was going to die. And yet I tried to help and it did no good. What was the point of my seeing it? What was the point of all that? I wish I'd never known."

"Don't you?" Argon asked. "But your knowing affected destiny. He was meant to be poisoned. You prevented that."

Thor stared back, puzzled. He had never thought of that.

"But he was killed anyway," Thor said.

"But not by poison. By dagger. And you don't know what effect that small change will have on the destiny of this kingdom."

Thor thought about that, his head hurting. It was too much for him to comprehend. He didn't fully understand what Argon was hinting at.

"The King wanted to see me before he died," Thor continued quickly, eager for answers. "Why me? Of all people? And what did he mean, when he spoke of my mother? Of my destiny being greater than his? Were these just the words of a dying man?"

"I think you know they were far more than that," Argon replied.

"So then it's true?" Thor asked. "My destiny is greater even than his? How is that possible? He was a king. I am nothing."

"Are you, then?" Argon asked back.

Argon took several steps forward, standing feet away from Krohn, and stared down at him. Krohn whined, and turned and ran away. Thor felt a chill, as Argon stared right through him.

"God does not choose the arrogant for his will. He chooses the humble. The least likely. Those overlooked by everyone else. Have you not considered this? All of your days farming, tending your father's sheep in your village. This is a warrior's—a true warrior's—foundation. Humility. Reflection. This is what forges a warrior. Did you never sense it? That you were greater than what you were? That you were meant for something else?"

Thor thought, and realized that he had sensed it.

"Yes," Thor responded. "I felt that…maybe I was meant for greater things."

"And now that they arrive, you still don't believe it?" Argon asked.

"But why me?" Thor asked. "What are my powers? What is my destiny? Where did I come from? Who was my mother? Why must everything in life be such a riddle?"

Argon slowly shook his head.

"One day, you will discover these things. But you have much to learn first. You must first become who you are. Your powers are deep, but you know not how to wield them. A mighty river flows within you, but it still lingers beneath the surface. You must bring it forward. You will learn much in your hundred days. But remember, that will be just the beginning."

Thor looked up at Argon, wondering how much he saw.

"I feel guilty to live," Thor said. He wanted desperately to tell Argon what was on his mind, the one person who could understand. "The king is dead, and yet I am alive. I feel that his death is on my head. And it hurts to go on."

Argon turned and looked at him.

"One king dies and another follows. That is the way of the world. A throne is not meant to sit empty. Kings will flow, like a river, through our Ring. All will seem permanent, and all will be fleeting. Nothing in this world—not you, not I—can stop the current. It is a parade of puppets, in the service of fate. It is a march of kings."

Thor sighed, looking out at the horizon for a very long time.

"The ways of the universe are inscrutable," he finally continued. "You will not understand them. Yes, it hurts to go on. But we must. We have no choice. And remember," he said, smiling at Thor with a smile that terrified him, "one day, you will join MacGil, too. Your time here is but a flash. Don't let life weigh you down with fear and guilt and regret. Embrace every moment of it. Do you understand me? The best thing you can do for MacGil now is to live. To *really* live. Do you understand me?"

Argon reached out and grabbed Thor by the shoulders, and it felt like two fires burning through his arms. He stared down with such intensity, Thor finally had to turn his head, and blink his eyes shut.

He raised up his hands to protect his eyes, and then suddenly, he felt nothing. He looked up. Argon was gone. Vanished.

Thor stood there alone in the field, turning in every direction. He saw nothing but the open sky, the open plains, and the howling of the wind.

*

Thor sat around the fire on the cool summer night, staring into the flames silently with the other Legion members as the wood cracked and popped. He leaned back on his elbows and looked up at the night sky, and in the distance, countless stars twinkled red and orange. Thor wondered, as he often did it, about distant worlds out there. He wondered if there were planets that weren't divided by canyons, seas that weren't protected by dragons, kingdoms that were not divided by armies. He wondered about the nature of fate and destiny.

The fire crackled, and he looked over at the roaring flames, around which sat his brothers-in-arms, hunched over, arms resting on their knees, looking somber and on-edge. Some of them roasted pieces of meat on sticks.

"Want one?" came a voice.

Thor turned and saw Reese, sitting beside him, holding out a stick wrapped in a white, gooey substance. He looked around and saw that they were being passed around to other boys around the fire.

"What is it?" Thor asked, as he took it and touched the white mass. It was sticky.

"Sap from the Sigil Tree. You roast it. Wait until it turns purple. It's delicious. And it will be the last tasty thing you have in a while."

Thor watched the other boys holding their sticks into the fire, watched as the white substance hissed. He held his out, too, into the flames, and was amazed as the substance bubbled over, then turned colors. It turned all the colors of the rainbow before it turned purple.

He pulled it out and tasted it, and was amazed at how good it was. It was sweet and chewy, and he took bite after bite.

Seated on his other side, chewing happily, were Elden, O'Connor, and the twins. As Thor looked around, he realized that the Legion fell into natural cliques. With the ages ranging from 14 to 19, and with nearly a hundred boys in the Legion, there were a dozen boys in each age range. The 19 year olds barely acknowledged the 14-year-olds, and each year seemed to stick to itself. Looking at the faces of the 19 year olds, Thor could hardly conceive how much older they looked, like full-grown men, compared to the boys his age. They looked almost too old to even still be in the Legion.

"Are they coming, too?" Thor asked Reese. He did not need to ask where. The Hundred was on everyone's mind this night, and no one seemed to think or talk of anything else.

"Of course," Reese answered. "Everyone goes. No exceptions. Every age range."

"The only difference," Elden interceded, "is that when they return, they are done with the Legion. It only goes to 19. And then they graduate."

"And then what?" Thor asked.

"If they make it through their final Hundred," Reese answered, "then they go before the King, and the King chooses which become Knights. Then, if they are chosen, the kingdom places them in posts for patrol duty throughout the kingdom. They have to do two years of rotation. Then they return to King's Court, and are eligible to join The Silver."

"Is it possible that they wouldn't pass the Hundred? After all these years?" Thor asked.

Reese furrowed his brow.

"It is different for every age and every year. I know stories of many who have not made it, at any age."

The group of boys fell silent, as Thor stared into the flames, wondering what lay ahead of them. After a long while, there was a commotion, and the boys turned to see Kolk marching into the center of the circle, his back to the flames, flanked by two warriors. Kolk scowled down at the boys, slowly pacing, looking each one in the eye as he went.

"Rest up, and eat up," he said. "This will be the last time you do. From here on, you're no longer boys, but men. You're about to embark on the hardest hundred days of your life. When you return—if you return—those of you who return will finally be worth something. Now, you're nothing."

Kolk continued pacing, walking slowly, looking as if he wanted to strike fear into each and every one of them.

"The Hundred is not a test," he continued. "It is not practice. It is real. What you do here, the sparring, the training—that is practice. But in the next hundred days, that is all gone. You will be entering a war zone. We are crossing the Canyon, will be beyond the shield, trekking for miles through the Wilds, into unguarded territory. We will be boarding ships, and crossing the Tartuvian Sea. We will be in enemy waters, far from the coast. We will be going to an island that is unmanned and unprotected from attack, in the heart of the Empire. We could be ambushed any time. There will be enemy forces all around us. And dragons lurk not far from there.

"Without fail, there will be battle. A few of us warriors will accompany you, but mostly you will be on your own. You will be men, forced to fight real men's battles. Sometimes to the death. This is how you learn battle. Each year, some of you will die. Some will be injured permanently. Some will drop out from fear. And the select few who return—those are the ones who merit joining the Legion. If you are too scared to go, don't show up tomorrow. Every year at this night, a few of you will pack up and leave. If that is you, I hope you do. We don't want cowards joining us."

With that, Kolk turned and stormed away, his men following.

A low whisper spread among the boys, as they looked solemnly at each other. Thor could see fear on many of their faces.

"Is it really that bad?" O'Connor asked a boy sitting beside him. The boy was older, maybe 18, and he stared into the flames, his wide jaw locked in a grimace.

He nodded.

"It is different every time," he said. "I've had many of my brothers not come back with me. Like he said, it's real. The best advice I can give you is to prepare for life-and-death. But I'll tell you one thing: if you make it back, you'll be a better warrior than you ever thought you could be."

Thor wondered if he could make it. Was he tough enough? How would he react when faced with real life and death combat? How could they sustain a hundred days of it? And what he would be like when he came back? He sensed that he would not return the same person. None of them would. And they would all be in it together.

He looked at Reese's face, and saw how distracted he was, and realized he was weighed down by something else. His father.

"I'm sorry," Thor said to him.

Reese did not look at him, but slowly nodded, his eyes welling, looking down at the ground.

"I just want to know who did it," Reese said "I just want to know who killed him."

"As would I," Elden echoed.

"And we," the twins echoed.

"Did he tell you anything?" Reese asked Thor. "In those last minutes with him? Did he tell you who did it?"

Thor could sense the others all looking at him. He tried to remember exactly what the king said.

"He told me he saw who did it. But he could not remember his face."

"But was it someone he knew?" Reese pressed.

"He said it was," Thor said.

"But that hardly narrows it down," O'Connor said. "A king knows more people than we ever will."

"I'm sorry," Thor added. "He didn't tell me anymore."

"But you were in there with him for minutes before he died," Reese pressed. "What else did he say to you?"

Thor hesitated, wondering how much to tell Reese. He didn't want to make him envious or jealous, or cause jealousy among the other boys. What could he possibly say? That the king said his destiny was greater than his? That would only stir the envy and hatred of everyone else.

"He did not say much," Thor said. "He was mostly silent."

"But then why did he want to see you? You specifically? Right before he died? Why did he not want to see me?" Reese pressed.

Thor sat there, not knowing how to respond. He realized how bad Reese must have felt, being his son, and having his father choose to see someone else in his final moments. He did not know what to say to comfort him, and had to think of something fast.

"He wanted me to tell you how much he cared for you," Thor lied. "I think it was easier for him to tell a stranger."

Thor felt Reese examining him to see if he was lying.

Finally, Reese turned and looked away, seeming satisfied. Thor felt bad not telling the complete truth. He hated to lie, and he never did. But he did not know what else to say. And he did not want to hurt his friend's feelings.

"And what of the sword now?" Conval asked.

Reese turned and looked at him.

"What do you mean?"

"You know what I mean. The Dynasty Sword. Now that the king is dead, the next MacGil will have a chance to try to wield it. I hear that Gareth is being crowned. Is that true?"

All the boys around the fire, even the older ones, grew quiet and looked at Reese.

Reese slowly nodded.

"It is," he said.

"That means Gareth will get to try," O'Connor said.

Reese shrugged.

"According to tradition, yes. If he chooses to."

"Do you think he'll be able to wield it?" Elden asked. "Do you think he is the One?"

Reese snorted in derision.

"Are you kidding? He's my brother by blood only. Not by choice. I have nothing to do with him. He is not the One. He is not even a King. He is barely a prince. If my father were alive, he would never be king. I would bet my life that he would be unable to wield that sword."

"And then how shall that look to the other kingdoms, if our new king should try and fail?" Conval asked. "Another failed MacGil king? It will make us seem weak."

"Are you saying that my father was a failure?" Reese snapped, on edge.

"No," Conval said, backing down. "I didn't meant that. I'm just saying that our kingdom will look weak if our new king fails to wield the sword. It could invite attack by others."

Reese shrugged.

"There is nothing we can do. When the right time comes, one day, a MacGil will wield that sword."

"Maybe it will be you," Elden said.

All the others turned and stared at Reese

"After all," Elden added, "you are the king's other true son."

"So is Godfrey," Reese answered. "He is also older than me."

"But Godfrey would never rule. And after Gareth, that leaves you."

"None of that matters," Reese said. "Gareth is king now. Not me."

"Maybe not for long," said one of the other boys, a deep voice from somewhere in the crowd.

"What do you mean?" Reese asked into the night, searching out the face.

But only silence came in return, as the others looked away.

"There are rumors of a revolt," Elden said finally. "Gareth is nothing like you. Nothing like us. He has made many enemies. Especially among the Legion, and among the Silver. Anything can happen. You might one day find yourself King."

Reese reddened.

"I would only wish to be king if it were legitimate. Not under those circumstances. Not because of my father's early death, and not because Gareth was betrayed. Besides, my eldest brother Kendrick would be far better than me."

"But he is not eligible," said O'Connor.

"Well then there is also my sister, Gwendolyn. That was my father's final wish."

"For a girl to rule?" someone yelled out in surprise. "That would never happen."

"But that was his wish," Reese insisted.

"But he shall not get his wish now, shall he?" someone remarked.

Slowly, Reese shook his head.

"For better or for worse, we're all in Gareth's hands now," he said.

"Who knows what we shall return to in a hundred days?" Elden remarked.

The group fell silent, as they all stared into the flames.

Thor sat there, thinking. The mention of Gwendolyn's name left a pit in his stomach. He turned and whispered to Reese.

"Your sister," he said. "Did you see her, after the funeral?"

Reese looked at Thor, and slowly nodded.

"We spoke. I cleared your name. She knows you had nothing to do in the brothel."

Thor felt a great sense of relief, felt his stomach relax for the first time in days. He was overwhelmed with gratitude towards Reese.

"Did she say she wants to see me again?" Thor asked, hopefully.

Reese shook his head.

"I'm sorry, my brother," he said. "She is a proud one. She does not like to admit when she's wrong. Even if she is."

Thor turned and looked back into the flames, and slowly nodded. He understood. He felt a hollowness in his stomach, but it gave him strength. There would be a long hundred days ahead of him, and it would be best if he had nothing left to care for.

*

Thor stood in the king's chamber, over his bed, the room dark save for a single torch at the far end that flickered slowly. Thor took three slow steps, knelt down beside the king, and held his hand. His eyes were closed. He looked peaceful. He was cold and still, and Thor could feel that he was dead.

MacGil's crown still sat on his head, and as Thor watched, Ephistopheles suddenly flew into the room, swooped down through an open window, and landed on the king's head. She grabbed the crown in her mouth, and flew away with it. She screeched as she flew out the window, her huge wings flapping, carrying the crown far into the sky.

Thor looked back at MacGil, and saw that now, in his place, lay Gareth. Thor quickly withdrew his hand, as he saw that Gareth's hand was that of a snake; he looked up and saw that Gareth's face was transforming, mixed with that of a cobra. He had scaly skin, and a tongue which flickered out at him. Gareth smiled an evil smile, his eyes flashing yellow.

Thor blinked, and when he opened his eyes, he found himself standing in his village, back home. The streets were deserted. The houses were all deserted, too, the doors and windows open, as if the entire village had left in haste.

Thor walked down the road he remembered, dust swirling all around him, until he arrived at his old house, a small, white clay dwelling, its door wide open.

He walked inside, ducking his head, and there, sitting at the table, his back to him, was his father. Thor walked around, his heart thumping, not wanting to see him again—but at the same time feeling compelled to.

Thor reached the far end of the table, and sat down at the other head, facing his father. His father's wrists were chained to the wood, with big iron shackles, and he stared sternly back.

"You have killed our king," his father said.

"I did not," Thor responded.

"You were never part of this family," his father said.

Thor's heart pounded, as he tried to process his father's words.

"I never loved you!" his father screamed, standing, breaking the shackles. He took several steps towards Thor, the shackles flailing. "I never wanted you!" he shrieked.

He charged Thor, raising his huge hands as if to choke him. Just as his hands closed in on Thor's throat, Thor blinked.

Thor stood at the head of a ship, a huge, wooden warship, its bow crashing deep into the ocean then rising high, waves crashing all around him. Thor stood at the helm, and before him flew Ephistopheles, still carrying the king's crown. In the distance there appeared an island, rising out from the sea, covered in a mist. And beyond that, a flame in the sky. The sky was filled with dark purple clouds, the two suns sitting near each other.

Thor heard a horrific roar, and he knew this was the Isle of Mist.

Thor woke with a start. He sat up breathing hard. He looked all around him, wondering.

It had been a dream. He was lying there, in the barracks, in the early light of dawn, the other boys sleeping all around him. His heart pounded as he wiped the sweat from his brow. It had seemed so real.

"I know something of bad dreams, boy," came a voice.

Thor spun and saw Kolk standing there, not far off, fully dressed, hands on his hips, looking down at the other boys.

“You’re the first to rise,” he said. “That is good. We have a long journey ahead of us. And your nightmares are just the beginning.”

CHAPTER ELEVEN

Gareth stood at his open window, watching dawn break over his kingdom. *His* kingdom. It felt good to think the words. As of today, he would be King. Not his father, but *he*. Gareth MacGil. The eighth of the MacGils. The crown would sit on his head.

It was a new era now. A new dynasty. It would be his face on the royal coins, a statue of *him* outside the castle. In just weeks, his father's name would be a memory, something relegated to the history books. Now it was *his* time to rise, *his* time to shine. It was the day he had looked forward to his entire life.

In fact, Gareth had been up all night, unable to sleep, tossing and turning, pacing the floors, sweating, covered in cold chills. In the few moments he had slept, he had had fast and troubled dreams, had seen the face of his father, staring back at him, reprimanding him, just as it had in life. But now his father could not touch him. Now *he* was in control. He had opened his eyes from sleep and made the face go away. He was in the land of the living, not his father. He and he alone.

Gareth could hardly conceive all the changes happening around him. As he watched the sky grow warmer, he knew that in just hours, he would wear the crown, the royal robe, wield the royal scepter. All the king's advisers, all the king's generals, all the people of his kingdom, would answer to *him.* He would control the Army, the Legion, the treasury. In fact, there was nothing he could not control, and there was not a single person who would not answer to him. It was the power he had sought, had craved, his entire life. And now it was in his grasp. Not in his sister's, and not in any of his brothers'. He had managed to make it happen. Perhaps prematurely. But he figured one day it would have been his anyway. Why should he have to wait his entire life, waste his prime, waiting? He should be king in his prime, not as an old man. He had just made it happen a bit sooner.

It was what his father deserved. His entire life he had criticized him, had refused to accept him for who he was. Now Gareth was *forcing* his father to accept him, from beyond the grave, whether he liked it or not. He was forcing him to have to look down and see his least loved son as ruler, the very son he had never wanted. That was his punishment for withdrawing his love, and for never giving him love to begin with. Gareth didn't need his love now. Now he had the whole kingdom to love and adore him. And he would squeeze out every ounce of it that he could.

There came a pounding on the door, the iron knocker resonating on the wood, and Gareth turned, already dressed, and strutted to the door. He yanked it open himself, marveling that this would be the last time he would do so. After today, he would sleep in a different room—the King's chamber—

and would have servants around the clock standing in and outside of his door. He would never touch a doorknob again. He would be flocked by a royal entourage, warriors, bodyguards, anything he wanted. He was electrified at the thought of it.

"My liege," came the chorus of voices.

A dozen of the king's guard bowed down as the door opened.

One of his advisers stepped forward.

"We have come to accompany you to the crowning ceremony."

"Very well," Gareth said, trying to sound composed, trying not to sound as if he had anticipated this moment every day of his life.

He walked forward, raising his chin, already trying to practice the look of a king. He would allow this day to change him, and he would demand that everyone around him look at him differently.

Gareth walked down the red carpet that had been laid out for him along the castle stone floor, dozens of guards lined up along it, awaiting his approach. He walked slowly and deliberately, turning down corridor after corridor, reveling each moment. Everywhere he went guards bowed low.

"My liege," they said, one after another, like dominoes.

It felt good to hear the words. It felt surreal. It felt as if he were walking in the footsteps that his father had walked just the day before.

As Gareth turned the corner, attendants opened a towering oak door, pulled with all their might on the iron knocker. It creaked open, revealing an immense ceremonial chamber. Gareth had expected a crowd, but he was taken aback by the site before him: there were thousands of the courts finest and most important people, nobles, royalty, hundreds of The Silver, all filling the room, all standing at his presence as the doors opened. They were lined up neatly in pews, dressed in their finest, as they would be for the most important ceremony. Thousands of them turned and faced him, and bowed their heads.

Gareth could hardly believe it. All of these people, all assembled just for him. It was too late now for anyone to stop him. The time had come. In just moments he would be wearing the crown, and that was a line that could never be crossed. His head itched to have it on.

He walked self-consciously down the long aisle, hundreds of feet with a plush red carpet down the middle. At its end sat an altar and a throne. Argon stood there waiting, with several more of the king's council.

"Hear ye hear ye! All rise in acceptance of the presence of the new King!"

"Hear ye!" came a chorus of shouts, thousands of voices filling the room, rising up to the cathedral ceiling. Music rose up, the sounds of a lute, as Gareth began the ceremonial walk to the throne. As he went, he passed faces that he recognized, and faces he did not. There were people that used to look at him as if he were just another boy, or who used to not look at him at all. Now they all had to pay him respect. Now he demanded all of their attention.

As he went he passed his siblings, standing together. Godfrey, Kendrick, Gwendolyn, and

Reese. Beside Reese was that boy, Thor. All of them, thorns in his side. No matter. He would do away with them soon enough. As soon as he assumed the throne, as soon as he took power, he would deal with each in his own way. After all, who better than he to know that the worst enemies are those closest to you.

Gareth passed his mother, the Queen, who stared down at him with a disapproving glance. He didn't need her approval now, or ever again. Now he was her King. Now she would have to answer to him.

Gareth continued to walk, passing everyone, until finally he reached the throne. The music grew louder as he ascended the seven ivory steps, to a platform where Argon was waiting, dressed in his finest ceremonial robes.

Gareth faced him. As he did, the entire room, thousands of people, sat. The music stopped and the room grew deathly still.

Gareth looked at Argon, who stared back at him with such intensity that his translucent eyes seemed to burn right through him. Gareth wanted to look away, but forced himself not to. He wondered again what Argon saw. Did he see the future? Or worse, did he see the past? Had he seen what Gareth had done? And if he had, would he reveal it?

Gareth made a mental note to oust Argon, too. He would oust anyone and everyone who had been close to his father—and who might suspect his guilt.

Gareth braced himself as Argon was about to open his mouth, praying he did not say anything to out him as the assassin.

"As the fates would have it," Argon announced slowly, "we are all put here on this day to mourn the loss of a great King, and to at the same time acknowledge the crowning of his son. For the law of the Ring dictates the kingship must be passed to the firstborn legitimate son. And that is Gareth MacGil."

Each and every one of Argon's words felt like a denunciation to Gareth. Why had he had to qualify it, to use the word *legitimate*? It was clearly a snub; he was clearly implying that he wished Kendrick could be king instead. Gareth would make him pay for that.

"As sorcerer to the MacGils for seven generations, it is my duty to place the royal crown on you, Gareth, in the hopes that you will carry out the supreme law of the kingship of the Ring. Do you, Gareth, accept this privilege?"

"I do," Gareth responded.

"Do you, Gareth, vow to uphold and protect the laws of our great kingdom?"

"I do."

"Do you, Gareth, promise to follow in the footsteps of your father, in all his ways, and in the footsteps of your ancestors, to protect the Ring, to uphold the Canyon, and to defend us from all enemies, internal and external?"

"I do."

Argon stared at him long and hard, expressionless, then finally reached over, picked up a large bejeweled crown, the one his father wore, raised it high, and slowly placed on Gareth's head. As he did, he closed his eyes and began to chant, over and over again, in the ancient, lost language of the Ring.

"*Atimos lex vi mass primus…*"

Argon chanted a deep, guttural chant, and it continued for some time. Finally, he stopped, reached up with his hand, and placed it on Gareth's forehead.

"By the powers vested in me by the Western Kingdom of the Ring, I, Argon, hereby name you, Gareth, the eighth MacGil King."

A muted applause rose up in the room, far from enthusiastic, and Gareth turned and faced all of his subjects. They all stood, politely, and Gareth looked over their faces.

He took two steps back and sat in his father's throne, sinking into it, feeling what it felt like to rest his hands on its well-worn arms. He sat there, staring at his subjects, who looked up at him with hopeful, maybe fearful eyes. He also saw in the crowd those who did not cheer, who looked at him skeptically.

He remembered their faces well, and each of them would pay.

*

Thor walked out of the king's castle, surrounded by Legion members, as they all filed out from the ceremony they had been forced to watch before their departure. He felt hollowed out. It made him physically sick to stand there and watch Gareth be crowned King. It was surreal. Just hours ago, MacGil had sat there, indomitable, on that throne, wearing that crown, holding that staff. Just hours ago, the entire kingdom had paid tribute to his father. Where had all their loyalty gone?

Of course, Thor understood that a kingdom had to have a ruler, and that a throne could not sit vacant for long. But could it not have sat vacant for just a little longer? Was it the nature of a throne that it could never sit empty for more than a few hours? What was it about a throne, about a kingship, about a title, that always made others rush to fill it? Was Argon right? Would there always be a march of kings? Would it ever end?

As Thor had watched Gareth sit in it, that throne seemed more like a gilded prison than a seat of power. It was not a seat, he realized, that he would ever want for himself.

Thor was reminded of MacGil's final words, about his destiny being greater than his. He shuddered; he prayed that he had not meant that he would ever be king—not here, not anywhere. Politics did not interest him. Thor wanted to be a great warrior. He wanted glory. He wanted to fight beside his brothers-in-arms, to help others in need. That was all. He wanted to be a leader of men in the realm of battle—but not outside of it. He could not help but feel that every leader who strived for power somehow ended up corrupted in the process.

Thor filtered out with the others, all of them upset that their journey had been delayed in order to pay homage to the new Prince. This day had been declared a national holiday, and now they could not all leave until the next morning. This left another day to do nothing but sit around, mourn the former king and contemplate Gareth's rise. It was the last thing Thor wanted. He had looked forward to journeying, to crossing the Canyon, to getting on the ship, to having the ocean air clear his senses, to leaving all of this behind and throwing himself into whatever training the Legion had in store for him.

As they exited the castle gates, Reese came up beside him and jabbed him hard in the ribs. Thor turned and saw Reese gesturing off to the side. Thor turned to look—and when he did, he could scarcely believe it.

There, standing off by herself, dressed in a long dress of black silk, stood Gwendolyn. She was looking right at him.

Thor could hardly comprehend it. He had thought that she had not wanted to see him again.

"She wants to speak with you," Reese said to Thor. "Go to her."

O'Connor, Elden and the twins, along with several other boys, let out a chorus of oohs and aahs, jostling Thor.

"Lover boy is being summoned!" O'Connor called out.

"Better run to her, before she changes her mind!" Elden said.

Thor, reddening, turned and looked at Reese, trying to ignore the others.

"But I don't understand. I thought she didn't want to see me."

Reese slowly shook his head, smiling.

"I guess she came around," he answered. "Go to her. We don't leave until tomorrow. You have time."

Thor heard a yelp and looked down to see Krohn take off, charging towards Gwendolyn. Thor needed no more prodding: he took off after him, to the mocking calls of his friends. Thor didn't care. Nothing mattered to him now, as his mind was filled with thoughts of seeing her. He had not realized how badly he had missed her, how deep a pain had sat in his chest, until he saw her again.

Thor followed Krohn as he zigzagged through the crowd, and finally reached her. She stood not far from the entrance to the castle, and he stood before her, jostled by the hundreds of people continue to filter out from the ceremony. She stood there, staring back, solemn. It saddened him to see the great joy that used to light up her face now gone, replaced with a withdrawn look, an aura of mourning. Yet somehow, it made her even more beautiful in the stark morning light. Krohn jumped on her foot, but she held her eyes on Thor's.

Now that he was standing before her, once again, he hardly knew what to say. He was about to speak, to say something, but she spoke first.

"I'm sorry for my words yesterday," she said, softly. "About you being a commoner. Being beneath me. I didn't mean it. I was just upset. It is unlike me. Forgive me."

Thor's heart swelled at her words. He could hardly believe she was being kind to him again.

"You don't need to apologize," he said.

"I do," she said. "I didn't mean those things. Reese told me all those things I heard about you were lies. I was mistaken. I should have known better than to listen to the others. I should have given you a chance."

She looked at him, her startling blue eyes mesmerizing him, and he found it hard to think straight.

"Will you give me another chance?" she asked.

Thor broke into a wide smile.

"Of course I will," he said. He looked down and kicked the rocks before him. "In fact, I hadn't given up hoping that you might change your mind. Because I never changed mine."

She looked up at him, and for the first time in a while she smiled, a broad smile, and it lifted Thor's heart. He felt a hundred pounds lighter.

All around them people continued to filter out and they were jostled every which way. She reached out and took his hand, and the feel of her smooth skin electrified him.

"Come with me," she said.

Thor could feel the looks of those all around them, and he wanted to leave, too.

"Where shall we go?" he asked.

"You'll see," she answered.

Without hesitation he followed, she guiding him as they held hands through the crowd, around the side of the castle, and out towards the open fields.

*

Thor and Gwen walked hand-in-hand in the early morning light through fields of flowers, Krohn at their side, the second sun rising, a beautiful summer day blooming around them. They passed through groves of trees, in full bloom with turquoise and white and green flowers, birds of all sorts swooping down around them. Flowers up to their knees, they continued climbing the gentle slope of a hill until finally they reached the top.

From up top, the view was magnificent. Thor turned, and had a sweeping view of the King's Court in every possible direction. It was a clear blue and yellow sky, a wisp of cloud sitting gently on the horizon.

Affecting Thor even more than the sweeping vista was the site he saw as he turned the other way: King MacGil's burial plot. Set against the dramatic Kolvian Cliffs was a fresh mound of dirt, a long pole marking it, with a circle at the end and a falcon within it, the symbol of their kingdom. There came a screech high up in the air, and as Thor watched, Ephistopheles swooped down and landed on the tip. She perched there, stared out at Thor and Gwen, and raised her wings and screeched again. She then lowered her wings and settled comfortably on the pole.

Thor and Gwen exchanged a puzzled look.

"The actions of animals will always be a mystery to me," Thor said.

"They sense things," she said. "They see things we do not."

Thor marveled that they were the only two here, at this fresh grave site. The thought of it pained him. But a day ago, the king could have commanded anyone he wanted, could have summoned thousands of people at his whim; now that he was dead, there was not a single person here to pay homage.

Gwen knelt down and gently placed the bunch of turquoise flowers she had picked along the way. Thor knelt beside her, smoothing the rocks away from the mound of dirt. Krohn walked up between them, lay down on the mound of dirt, lowered his chin, and whimpered.

As Thor knelt there, the only sound that of the whipping wind, he felt an overwhelming sense of grief. Yet, in a strange way, he also felt comforted. This was where he wanted to be. With MacGil. With Gwen. Not in the court, watching the prince be crowned. Not anywhere else.

"He knew his death was coming," she said.

Thor glanced over and saw Gwen, staring down at the grave, was tearing up.

"He sat me down, just days ago, and kept talking about his death. It was strange. It upset me. I told him to stop. But he wouldn't. Not until I promised him."

"Promised him what?" Thor asked.

Gwen, silent, wiped a tear, arranging the flowers perfectly on her father's mound of dirt. After a longtime, she finally leaned back, and sighed.

"He made me vow that if he died, I would rule his kingdom."

She turned and looked at Thor, her beautiful blue eyes wet, lit up in the morning sun, the most beautiful thing he'd ever seen, and he was shocked to realize her words were true.

"You? Rule the kingdom?" he asked, stunned.

Her face darkened.

"Do you not think I'm able?" she demanded.

Thor stammered.

"No—no—of course not. I didn't mean it that way. I—I was just surprised. I had no idea."

Her expression softened.

"I was surprised, too. It was not something I wanted. But I told him I would. He would not stop until I vowed."

"So…then I don't understand," Thor said, confused. "Why was Gareth crowned? Why not you?"

She looked back down towards her father's grave.

"My father's wish was never ratified. The Council would not abide by it."

"But that is not fair," Thor yelled out, feeling the indignity of it rising within. "It was not what your father wanted!"

She shrugged.

"Is just as well," she said. "It is truly not something I want."

"But it is not just that Gareth should be the one to rule."

She sighed, wiping back a tear, collecting herself.

"They say that each kingdom gets the king that it deserves," she said.

Her words lingered in the air, and as Thor really thought about that, he realized that Gwen was much wiser than he thought. He realized in that moment what a good ruler she would, in fact, make. It upset him all the more that she was passed over, that her father's wish was ignored.

"But I do worry for our kingdom," she said, "our half of the Ring. The McClouds—when they hear that Gareth is crowned—they will be emboldened. It will embolden all of our enemies. Gareth is not a ruler, and they all know that. We will be vulnerable."

Thor wondered about all the ramifications of the King's assassination. They seemed endless.

"But what bothers me most of all, is not knowing who killed him," she said. "I must know. I cannot rest until I do. I feel that my father's soul will not rest, either. Justice must be done. I don't trust anyone in this court. There are too many spies, and everyone lies. In fact, you're the only one I can really trust—and that is because you are an outsider. Along with my brothers, Kendrick and Reese. Other than that, I trust no one."

"Do you have any idea who might have wanted him killed?" Thor asked.

"I have many ideas. And many leads to pursue. I will pursue each one of them, and I will not stop until I find his killer."

Gwen was looking at her father's grave as she said it, and Thor felt the conviction in her words, felt that she would find out who did it.

After a long while, Gwen stood. Thor rose, too, and they stood there together, side by side, looking down at the grave.

"I want to get far away from here," Gwen said. "I want to leave this place. A part of me wants to never come back. I hate all of this. I don't know where it will all end. But I feel that it must all end tragically. In death. Betrayal. Assassination. I hate this court. I hate being royalty. I wish I could live a simple life. In fact, I wish my father had been a farmer. Then, he would still be alive. And that would mean more to me than the entire kingdom."

Thor, feeling her pain, reached out his hand and held hers. She did not pull away.

"I will be far from here myself, soon," he said.

She turned and looked to him, and he could see fear in her eyes.

"What do you mean?" she asked, urgently.

"Tomorrow we all embark, the entire Legion. The Hundred. We sail for training, for a distant isle. I won't be back until the Fall. Assuming I make it back at all."

Gwen looked crestfallen. She slowly shook her head.

"Life can be so cruel," she said. "Everything at once." She suddenly looked determined. "When does the ship sail?"

"In the morning."

She clasped his hand.

"That gives us a day together," she said, a smile forming. "Let's make the most of it."

Thor smiled back.

"But how?" he asked.

She smiled wider.

"I know the perfect place."

She turned and led him away, and the two of them took off, holding hands, running back through the fields, Krohn beside them. Thor had no idea where she was taking him, but as long as he was with her, nothing else mattered.

*

As Thor and Gwendolyn strolled through fields of flowers, up and down gentle hills, he marveled at how good it felt to be with her. He sensed her joy, too. It wasn't the joy she used to wear, that over-ebullient laugh and smile that lit up everything around her. That had been replaced by something more somber, more austere, since the death of her father.

They walked through fields bursting with color, a rainbow of pinks and greens and purples and whites, and Krohn ran around them, in circles, yelping and jumping, seeming even more happy than they. Finally they came to a large hill, and as they reached its top, Gwen stopped, and Thor did, too. He stopped, awestruck at the sight before him: there, on the horizon, sat a huge lake, made of a white-blue water, clearer than any water he had ever seen, sparkling beneath the sun. It was surrounded by towering mountains, and their cliffs looked alive, sparkling all different colors in the morning sunlight.

"The Lake of the Cliffs," she said. "It is ancient. It is a hidden lake; no one ever comes here. I discovered it when I was a child. I had too much time on my hands, and I would explore. Do you see that small island, there?" she asked, pointing.

Thor squinted into the sun, shimmering off the lake, and he saw it. A small island sat in the center of the lake, far from shore.

"It is where I would escape as a child. I would take that small boat, there," she said, pointing to a weathered rowboat on shore, "and row out myself.

Sometimes I would spend entire days on it, far from everyone. It was a place where no one could get to me. It is the only place left for me that is pure."

She turned and looked at Thor, and he looked at her. Her eyes were glowing, all different shades of blue, and they seemed truly alive for the first time since her father had died.

"I would like to take you there," she said. "I would like to share it with you."

Thor felt deeply touched, closer to her than he ever had.

"I would love to," he said.

She took his hand, and leaned in, and he leaned in, too, and their lips met. It was a magical kiss, the sun emerging from behind a cloud as they did, and he felt his entire being warm over. Her lips were smooth, and he reached up and felt her cheek, which was even smoother.

They held the kiss for a long time, until finally she pulled away and smiling, took his hand. The two of them began to walk down the hill, sloping gently down towards the shore of the lake, towards the small boat that sat there, waiting. Thor could hardly wait.

*

Thor rowed the small boat as Gwendolyn sat opposite him, across the tranquil white-blue waters of the lake, and as they crossed it, he rowed them right up onto the sandy shore of the small island, its sand sparkling red. Thor jumped out, pulled the boat up safely, then reached out and took Gwen's hand and helped her off. Krohn leapt out with an excited yelp, and began running on the sand.

Thor took Gwen's hand, and she lead the way as the two of them began hiking on the small island, the sand quickly giving way to a small field of grass and flowers. The island was alive with the sound of swaying trees, towering, exotic trees which leaned all the way over, the summer breezes rocking them left and right. As they swayed they dropped down small, white flower petals, falling like snow all around them. Gwen was right: this place was magical.

Gwen giggled, her spirits clearly lifted to be here; she took Thor's hand and led him on a small trail through the winding green paths. He could tell from how she walked that she knew every inch of this island by heart, and he wondered where she was taking him.

They twisted and turned, up-and-down trails, Thor ducking his head here and there to avoid branches, until finally she lead them to a small clearing, hidden by trees, in the center of the island. Thor was surprised to see that in its center sat the ruins of a small, crumbling stone structure, its walls still standing, but its inside hollowed out long ago. It was open to the elements on all sides, and its floor was comprised of a thick, soft moss. Inside there was a small mound of earth which curved gently upward, providing a small, naturally inclined bed.

Gwen led Thor, and they lay down on it, beside each other, their backs resting on the slope, looking up at the sky. Krohn ran over and lay down beside Gwen, and as she giggled and petted him, Thor was starting to wonder if Krohn liked Gwen more than he. As Thor leaned back, resting his head in his palms on the soft moss and looked up, high above him Thor could see the two suns, the bright turquoise and yellow sky, trees swaying in the wind, white flower petals falling. The sound of the breezes whipped through the place, and he felt for a moment like they were the only ones left. He felt as if they had escaped from the worries of the world, that they were in a safe, protected place, a place where no one could touch them. He felt more relaxed than he'd ever had, and wanted to never leave.

Beside them, he felt fingers on his, and looked over to see Gwen's hand. They locked fingers, and the touch of her skin made him feel even more deeply at ease. He felt that everything was right in the world.

As they lay there in the silence, feeling ever more deeply relaxed, he thought of his having to leave the following day—and the thought pained him. As excited as he had been to go, now, the thought of leaving Gwen upset him. With all that had gone on, with her father's death, with their misunderstanding and their reconciliation, finally, he felt like they were in a good place. He wondered if leaving would upset that. And he wondered what things would be like a hundred days from now, and whether she would still care for him.

"I wish I did not have to leave you tomorrow," he said. He found himself nervous to say it, hoping he did not sound too desperate.

But to his surprise, she turned and looked right at him, her face alight with a smile.

"I was hoping you would say that," she said. "I have been able to think of nothing else since you told me. The idea of your leaving pains me in a way I cannot describe. Seeing you again was the one thing that gave me solace."

She squeezed his hand, leaned in and kissed him, and he kissed her back. They kissed for a long time, then lay side-by-side again.

"And what of your mother?" Thor asked. "Will she still forbid your seeing me?"

She shrugged.

"Since my father's death, she's a different person. I don't recognize her anymore. She hasn't spoken a word to anyone. She just stares. I think a part of her died with him. I can't imagine her rousing to stop us. And if she does, I no longer care. I am my own person. I will find a way. I will leave this place if I have to."

Thor was surprised.

"You would leave the royal court? For me?"

She looked at him and nodded, and he could see the love in her eyes. He could see that it was true, and his heart swelled with gratitude.

"But where could we go?" he asked.

"Anywhere," she said. "As long as I am with you."

His heart soared at her words. He couldn't believe she had said that, because he had been thinking the same exact thing.

"Isn't it funny," she said softly, "how certain people come into your life at a certain time? You, coming into my life just as my father died. It is strange. I don't know what I would've done if you weren't here. And to think I almost lost you, and over a silly misunderstanding."

"I often wonder that myself," Thor answered. "What if I hadn't met Argon that day in the forest? What if I had not tried to come to King's Court, to join the Legion? What if I had never met you? How would my life be different?"

A long, comfortable silence fell between them.

"It's hard to fathom that in a day you will be so far from here," she said. "On a ship, on an ocean, in a distant land, under a different sky."

She sat up and turned and looked to him, fierceness in her eyes.

"Do you promise that you will come back for me?" she asked, with a sudden urgency. He could see how deeply she felt things. But it did not scare him—he was the same way.

He looked at her with equal seriousness.

"I promise," he answered.

"Vow to me," she said. "Vow that you will come back. That you will not leave me here. That, no matter what, you will return for me."

She held out her hands, and Thor took hers, and looked into her eyes with a seriousness to match hers.

"I vow," he answered. "I will come back for you. No matter what."

She looked into his eyes for a long time, then leaned in and kissed him. It was a long, passionate kiss, and he reached up and held her cheeks, pulling her close. He tried to ingrain in his memory the feel of her skin, the sound of her voice, the smell of her hair, tied to hold it in his mind so that even in a hundred days, he would not forget it. But his new powers arose within him, and a sixth sense was whispering to him. It was telling him, even in this moment, even at the height of his greatest joy, that something dark would come between them. And that the vow he had just made might cost him his life.

CHAPTER TWELVE

Erec rode from the rising of the first sun to the time the second crossed the sky when the country path widened, gradually became finer, smoother, the rough holes less frequent. Its jagged rocks were replaced by fine pebbles, then these replaced by smooth, white shells, and Erec knew he was, finally, approaching a city. He started to see people pass him on foot, carrying goods and wares, sheltering their heads with wide hats from the summer heat. The road become more and more populated, people passing him in both directions on this glorious summer day, some leading oxen or riding on carts. Judging from the number of days he had ridden, Erec assumed he was nearing Savaria, the stronghold of the South. It was a city famed for its fine women, its strong wine and its magnificent horses, one that Erec had heard much about, but had never had a chance to visit. It was famed, also, for its annual jousting competition, the prize for the winner being the bride of his choice. Women gathered from all over the Ring hoping to be picked, and knights of fame and honor poured in from all the provinces, hoping to win.

Erec figured it would be a good place to begin his Selection year. He did not expect to find his bride here, so soon, but he thought, at the very least, it would keep his jousting skills sharp. Being the king's hand, the finest knight in the kingdom, Erec had no doubt he could defeat any adversary. It was not hubris, just knowledge of his own skills compared to others. It had been years since he had been defeated by anyone. Whether he could find his bride was a different story.

Erec climbed a hill and as he reached its peak saw, spread out below him, a great city, with castles, parapets, spires, steeples and a brook running before it. It was framed by an ancient wall, as thick as two men. Savaria. It was a beautiful city, quaint, not nearly the size of King's Court, yet still substantial. It was built low to the ground, its buildings all made of stone, with slate roofs and smoke rising from chimneys. As Erec stopped on his horse, taking in the site, he spotted a lookout, high up on one of the towers, a boy dressed in the red and green colors of the South. The boy jumped to his feet, waved frantically towards Erec, and blew a long trumpet. It was the official greeting of the King's Guard, and as Erec watched, the metal gate beyond the drawbridge was raised. There was an excited shout, and two horses came galloping out towards him.

It occurred to Erec that members of The Silver rarely journeyed this far South, and that the arrival of one would be hailed as a major event—especially one coming right from King's Court. And the fact that it was Erec—the most celebrated of all The Silver, and the King's champion—would create an even greater stir. He could already see, even from here, the excitement in the boy's eyes, the gathering crowd on the towers, the anticipation in the soldiers galloping out to greet him.

The soldiers pulled to a stop before him, their horses breathing hard, and greeted him with smiles from behind the friendly red beards of the Savarians.

"My Liege," one of them called out. "A great honor to have you here! We have had no visitors from King's Court in years."

"What brings you to us?" asked the other. "Is it the festival?"

"It is," Erec responded. "It is my Selection Year, and I'm afraid I've been too picky."

The soldiers both laughed in response.

"That I can understand," one of them said. "I failed to choose by my year, as well, and also failed to find one during my Selection year. Thus I was assigned a bride. I lament it to this day!" he said with a hearty laugh. "Not a day passes when she doesn't nag me to death, that she does not remind me that I did not choose her!"

Erec laughed.

"My selection year comes up next season," said the other soldier. "I hope to find someone before then."

"Well I've just begun my journey," Erec said. "I don't know that I will find my bride here. But I would like to see your city. And I will join the tournament."

"Very well, my Liege," one of them said good-naturedly. "Our Duke will be thrilled at your presence. It would be a great honor if we can accompany you. You must understand that the arrival of the King's hand is a major event! You will be treated like royalty within our gates!"

Erec laughed.

"I am hardly royalty," he said, humbly. "I am just another knight."

"Hardly, my liege," the other said. "We've heard tales of your conquests far and wide."

"I just perform my duty to the king. Nothing else. But that said, I would be honored for you to accompany me. Let us to the Duke!"

The three of them turned and began trotting down the road, to the looks of wonder of the growing crowd, amassing along the roadway to catch a glimpse of Erec.

As they rode through the massive arched stone gate of Andalusia, Erec was struck by the throngs of people that came out to see him. They rode into the city center, a wide stone plaza, framed by ancient stone walls, and as they did, the Duke rode out to greet him, flanked by a dozen men. Approaching with them were dozens of women, dressed in their finest, standing before Erec, hoping to catch his eye. Each was more beautiful than the next. Erec could hardly believe it. All this attention, just for him. It made him feel more famous than he felt entitled to.

As the Duke approached, Erec remembered him—he had met him once, at King's Court, at a royal event. He was a tall and lean man, with a perfectly straight posture and a gallant look. Beside him, Erec was happy to see, was one of his brothers-in-arms, a member of The Silver, a man Erec had fought with on many occasions; they had been in the same year in the Legion, and seeing him brought back old memories. They had gotten into trouble together one too many times. Brandt. With his warm, green eyes and blond beard, Brandt looked exactly as he had when Erec had last seen him years ago.

Brandt's face lit up in a smile as he jumped down from his horse along with the Duke. Erec jumped down from his, and Brandt hurried up to him.

"Erec, you son of a mother's whore!" Brant called out with a hearty laugh. "I never thought I'd see you more than a hair's breadth from King's court!"

Brandt embraced him heartily.

"And I never thought I'd see you either, old friend."

"We are thrilled to have you here!" the Duke said, embracing him with a hearty clasp of the forearm. "It has been many years since we last met. You are most welcome here. Having you here is like having the King himself!

"GUARDS!" the Duke turned and yelled over his shoulder.

Several guards rushed forward.

"Prepare the banquet hall! We shall all have a glorious feasts tonight, in honor of our brother Erec!"

"Here here!" came a happy cheer from the crowd.

"And what brings you here?" Brandt asked. "Has the King sent you this way?"

"He has not, I'm afraid. I am on a…personal mission this time."

Brandt examined him, bunching his eyebrows; then his face lit up.

"Don't tell me," Brandt said. "You dog! You made it to your Selection year! You didn't choose anyone, did you? You son of a whore! I knew it! I knew you wouldn't! You were always more interested in swords than ladies. I never understood what you were waiting for. Half the women in King's Court threw themselves at your feet."

Erec laughed.

"I don't know what I've been waiting for either, my friend. But you are right, and here I am. I thought I might join your tournament."

"Oh!" they both yelled out.

"Will you compete, then?" the Duke asked. "In that case, our games are already over! For who could defeat you in battle?"

"*I* can give him a run for his money!" Brandt called out. "In fact, last I remember, I was beating you on the Legion's field."

Erec laughed.

"Were you, then?" Erec asked.

"Yes, we were ten years old. And you didn't stand a chance!" Brandt yelled.

Erec laughed.

"I haven't beat you since then—but then again, no one has, so I don't feel so bad. But I can always have a second chance now, can't I?" Brandt asked with a laugh.

Brandt draped an arm around Erec and turned and led him through the crowd, on foot, towards the castle. The Duke and his men fell in beside them.

"Out of the way, you Ruffians!" Brandt called out good-naturedly. "We have a real member of The Silver here!"

Erec laughed. It was good to see his old friend again.

"You might be the better fighter, but I can still drink you under the table!" Brandt said as they went.

"We shall have to see about that," Erec said.

"Your joining our competition shall be news indeed," the Duke said. "Most of all for these ladies. Look at them. Every single one stares at you. After all, they've come from all corners of the Ring to find a husband—and you will be the most eligible of all!"

"At tonight's feast," Brandt added, "you will get to see them up close. They will all be there. You will have your choice. You will name one tonight, I hope! Yes, that will make our games much, much more interesting!"

As they continued through the crowd, past the dozens of women, past the other knights trying to catch a glimpse of their new competition, Erec was happy to be at his old friend's side, and he felt very welcome. He looked forward to the night's festivities, especially after a hard day's ride. He also felt overwhelmed: he wasn't sure he was ready to pick a bride tonight.

But as he passed one beautiful woman after the next, he could not help but feel that tonight would be the night when everything changed.

CHAPTER THIRTEEN

Godfrey sat before the bar in the small tavern early in the day, the drinks already getting to his head. This had been the worst week he could remember. First, there was his father's death and funeral; then, there was his brother Gareth's crowning ceremony. He needed a drink. After all, what better way to toast a brother he hated? What better way to say goodbye to a father who had hated and disapproved of him his entire life?

As Godfrey sat there, flanked on either side by two of his drinking fellows, Akorth, a towering, burly fat man past his prime, with a wild red beard, and Fulton, a thin, older man with a voice that was way too raspy and a face prematurely aged by drink, Godfrey found himself surprised by his own feelings of despair. He had always thought that the day his father died would be a day of rejoicing, the day that the oppressor had finally been lifted off his shoulders, the day that he was finally free to drink, to live his way of life, without repercussions. In a way, it was. He felt some sense of relief, of liberation, no longer having his father around to disapprove of him. He felt freer to spend his life as he wished, to drink all day long without fear of recrimination.

But at the same time, to his surprise, he felt an unexpected feeling of remorse. There must have been something deep within him, something he had suppressed, something even he didn't realize, which bubbled up within him. He could hardly believe it, but he had to admit that a part of him was sad that his father was dead. A part of him actually wished he were still alive, and wished, more than anything, that he could have his approval. That just for one moment, his father would accept him for who he was, on his own terms. Even if he were nothing like him.

Oddly enough, Godfrey did not feel free, either. He had always expected that the day his father died, he would feel free to drink even more, to lock himself in the tavern with his friends. But now that he was dead, oddly, Godfrey no longer felt as much of a desire to drink. There was something inside him he had never experience before, some desire to go out and *do* something. Something responsible, he did not know what. It was weird, but there was a part of him that actually felt what it was like to be in his father's shoes.

"Another!" Akorth shouted to the bartender, who hurried over with three new casks of ale, the foam bubbling over, and slipped one into Godfrey's hands.

Godfrey lifted it to his mouth and drank long and hard, gulping it all down, feeling it rush to his head. He looked around and noticed that they were the only three in the bar, and he was not surprised, given it was still morning. He already wanted this day to end.

Godfrey looked down, saw the soil on his shoes from his father's burial, and felt the sadness re-igniting within him. He could not get the image out of his head of his father's body being lowered into the earth. It made him think of his own mortality, of how he had spent his life, and how he would spend the rest of it. More than anything, it made him realize how he had wasted his life. He was still young, only eighteen, but a part of him felt it was too late, that he was who he was. Was it, really? Or was there still any hope for him to turn his life around? To become the son his father always wanted him to be?

"Do you think it's too late for me?" he asked Akorth, turning towards him as he set down his cask. Akorth finished a cask with one hand then raised a fresh cask with another. He finally set it down and let out a loud belch.

"What do you mean?"

"To become an upstanding citizen. A warrior. Or anything worthwhile. If I ever wanted to. Something along those lines."

"You mean, do something responsible and worthwhile with your life?" he asked.

"Yes."

"You mean, to become one of *them*?" Fulton chimed in.

"Yes," Godfrey said. "If I wanted to. Do you think it's too late?"

Akorth let out a huge laugh, shaking the bar with it, slamming his palm on the table.

"All this business really got to you boy, didn't it?" Akorth bellowed. "It scares me to hear you speak this way. Why would you want to be one of them? I couldn't think of anything more boring."

"You live the good life in here, with us," Fulton said. "We have our whole lives ahead of us. Why waste time being responsible, when you can waste time drinking?"

Fulton screamed with laughter at his own joke, and Akorth joined in.

Godfrey turned back, looked down at his cask, and wondered if they were right. A part of him agreed with them: after all, that was the line he had always taken, the way he had always rationalized his existence. But he could not deny that a new part of him was starting to wonder if maybe there was something else. If maybe he'd had enough of all of this.

Most of all, what burned inside him was a sense of anger. And, oddly, a desire for vengeance. Not just against his father, but against his father's killer. Maybe it was just a desire to understand. He wanted—he needed—to know who killed his father. Who would want his father dead? Why? How had they got past all the guards? How could they not remain caught?

Godfrey turned over and over in his mind all the possibilities, all the people that might want him dead. For some reason, he kept thinking of his brother. Gareth. He kept thinking of that meeting, the one he had left so abruptly, with all his siblings, when his father had named a successor. He had heard that after he'd left, his father had named Gwendolyn. It was actually probably the only wise choice of his father's life—and probably the only thing Godfrey respected him for. Godfrey despised Gareth: he was an evil, plotting schemer. It was the wisest thing his father had ever done to cut him out of kingship. And yet now, look where they were. Gareth was crowned.

Something tugged away at Godfrey, something that would not disappear, that made him wonder more about him. There was some look of hate in Gareth's eyes, something he had spotted since he was a child. He couldn't help but wonder if Gareth had something to do with their father's murder. In fact, a part of him felt sure that he did. He did not know why. And he knew that no one would take him seriously, he, Godfrey, the drunk.

Still, a part of him felt compelled to find the answer. Maybe if for no other reason than to make amends to his father, to make up for his wasted life. If he could not have his father's approval in life, perhaps he could gain it in death.

Godfrey sat there, rubbing his head, trying to think, trying to get to the bottom of something. Something weighed on the dark corners of his consciousness, some message, persistently nagging at him. It was an image; maybe a memory. But he could not recall precisely of what. He knew, though, that it was important.

As he sat there, racking his brain, drying to drown out the laughter of the others, suddenly, it came to him. The other day. In the forest. He had spotted Gareth. With Firth. The two of them, walking. He remembered thinking at the time that it was strange. And he remembered that they had no answer for where they were going, or where they had been.

He suddenly sat upright, electrified. He turned to Akorth.

"Do you remember the other day, in the wood? My brother, Gareth?"

Akorth furrowed his brow, clearly trying to summon it through his drunken haze.

"I remember seeing him walking with that lover boy of his!" Akorth mocked.

"Hand-in-hand, I suspect!" Fulton chimed in, then burst into laughter.

Godfrey tried to concentrate, in no mood for their jokes.

"But do you recall where they were coming from?"

"Where?" Akorth asked, perplexed.

"You asked them, and they didn't tell you," Fulton said.

An idea was solidifying in Godfrey's brain.

"Odd, isn't it? The two of them walking there, in the middle of nowhere? Do you remember what he was wearing? A cloak and a hood on a hot summer day? Walking so fast, as if he was heading somewhere? Or coming from somewhere?"

Godfrey was convincing himself as he spoke.

Akorth looked at him, puzzled.

"What is it you're trying to put together?" he asked. "Because if you're asking me to figure it out, you've come to the wrong man, my friend. I would just tell you that if you want to get to the bottom of something, drink another ale!" he shouted, and roared with laughter.

But Godfrey was serious. He was focused. This time, he would not be distracted.

"I think he was going somewhere," Godfrey added, thinking out loud. "I think they were both going somewhere. And I think it was with ill intent."

He turned and stared at his two friends.

"And I think it has something to do with my father's death."

Akorth and Fulton finally stopped and looked at him, the smiles dropping from their faces.

"That's quite a leap," Akorth said.

"Are you accusing your brother and his lover of killing the King?" Fulton asked.

The bartender stopped in his tracks and stared, too.

Godfrey sat there, working it out, his mind reeling, feeling electrified, feeling a sense of purpose, of mission. It was a feeling he wasn't used to.

"That is exactly what I'm saying," he finally responded.

"That's dangerous talk," the bartender warned. "Your brother is king now. Someone hears you say that, you can go to the clink."

"My *father* is King," Godfrey corrected, steel in his voice, feeling himself overcome with a new strength. "My brother Gareth just had a crown put on his head. He is not a king. He is a prince, just like I. And a failed one at that."

The bartender slowly shook his head and looked away.

"Where were they going? What is out there, in that wood?" Godfrey asked Akorth with a sudden urgency, grasping his wrist.

"Calm down, my good man, there's no need to get upset—"

"I said, what is out there?" Godfrey demanded, shouting.

Akorth stared back at him with a look he had never seen before. One of shock. And maybe, even, of respect.

"What's gotten into you? I don't have answers for you. I have no idea."

"Wait a minute, there *is* something out there," Fulton said.

Godfrey turned and looked at him.

"Not there, exactly. But near there. Blackwood. A few miles away. There are rumors of a witch's cottage."

"A witch's cottage?" Godfrey repeated, slowly. The thought of it hit him like a spear.

"Yes. So the rumor goes. Do you think that's where they were going?"

Godfrey stumbled up from his barstool, knocking it over, and hurried across the room. His two friends jumped up, too, hurrying after him.

"Where are you going?" Akorth called out. "Have you lost your mind?"

Godfrey yanked open the door, the harsh morning light hitting his face, making him feel alive for the first time in he did not know how long. He stopped and turned and looked inside the ale house one final time.

"I'm going to find my father's murderer."

CHAPTER FOURTEEN

Steffen cowered beneath the whip of his master, bending over and bracing himself as he was lashed across the back yet again. He braced his hands over the back of his head, trying to shield the worst of the blow.

"I ordered you to remove the chamber when it was full! Now look at the mess you've made!" his master screamed.

Steffen hated to be yelled at. Born deformed, his back twisted in a permanent hunch, looking prematurely old, he had been yelled at from the time he was a child. He had never fit in with his siblings, with his friends, or with anyone. His parents had tried to pretend he didn't exist, and when he was just old enough, they found a reason to kick him out of the house. They had been embarrassed by him.

Since then, it had been a hard, lonely life for Steffen, left to fend for himself. After years of working odd jobs, of begging in the streets when he needed to, he had finally found a job in the bowels of the king's castle, toiling with the other servants in the room of the chamber pots. His task, for years, was to wait until the huge, iron chamber pot was filled with sewage from the floors above, then carry it out while it was overflowing, with the help of another servant. They took it out the back door of the castle, across the fields, to the river's edge, and dumped it in.

It was a job he had over the years learned to do well, and as his posture was ruined before he arrived, the lugging of the pot could not have affected it anymore. Of course, the stench of the waste was unbearable, though, over time, he had learned to block it out. He had taught his mind go to other places, to escape in fantasy, to imagine vivid alternate worlds and to convince himself that he was anywhere but here. Steffen's one gift in life had been a great imagination, and it didn't take much to send him off to another realm. His other great gift was observation. Everyone underestimated him, but he heard and saw everything, and he took it all in like a sponge. He was much more sensitive and perceptive than people realized.

Which was why, the other day, when that dagger had come tumbling down the stone chute, into the chamber pot, Steffen had been the only one to take notice. He heard the slightest difference in the splash, something landing in the water that sounded not human, but metal. He'd heard the tiniest bit of a clang as it settled to the bottom—and he had known immediately that something was wrong. Something was different. Somebody had dropped something down the chute, something he wasn't supposed to. Either it was an accident, or, more likely, it was on purpose.

Steffen waited for a moment when the others weren't looking and stealthily approached the pot, held his nose, rolled up one sleeve, and reached in up to his shoulder. He fished around until he had found it. He had been right: there was something there. It was long and metal, and he grasped it and pulled it up. He could feel, before it even reached the surface, that it was a dagger. He extracted it quickly, glanced it over, made sure no one was looking, and bundled it in a rag and hid it behind a loose brick.

Now that things had quieted down, he looked around, made sure no one was looking, and when he felt sure the coast was clear, he hurried over to the brick, loosened it, unwrapped the weapon and studied it. It was a dagger unlike any he had ever seen, certainly not one for the lower classes. It was an aristocratic thing, a piece of art. Very valuable, and expensive.

As he held it up to the torchlight, turning it every which way, he noticed stains on it, stains which would not come out. He realized, with a shock, that they were blood stains. He remembered back to when the blade had fallen down and realized that it had come down on the same night of the assassination of the King. His hands shook as he realized he might be holding the murder weapon.

"How stupid are you?" shrieked his master, as he whipped him again.

Steffen hunched over and quickly wrapped up the blade, keeping his back to his boss, hoping and praying he had not seen it. He had left the chamber pot untended while examining the blade, and it had overflowed. He had not expected his master to be so close.

Steffen took the beating, as he did every day, whether he did a good job or not. He clenched his jaw, hoping it would end soon.

"If that pot overflows again, I will have you kicked out of here! No, worse, I will have you chained and thrown in the dungeon. You stupid deformed hunchback! I don't know why I put up with you!"

His master, a fat, pockmarked man with a lazy eye, reached up and beat him again and again. Usually, the blows ended; but tonight he seemed to be in a particularly belligerent mood and the blows just kept getting worse. They never seemed to end.

Finally, something inside Steffen snapped. He could stand it no longer.

Without thinking, Steffen reacted: he grasped the hilt of the dagger, spun around and plunged it into his master's rib cage.

His master let out a horrified gasp as his eyes bulged in his head. He stood there, frozen, looking down in wonder.

Finally, the blows stopped.

Now Steffen was furious. All the pent up anger he'd felt over the years came pouring out.

Steffen grimaced, grabbed his master by the throat, and squeezed it with one hand. With the other, he pushed the blade in deeper and slowly dragged it higher, cutting him up through the sternum, all the way to his heart. Hot blood poured out over his hand and wrist.

Steffen was shocked at what he had summoned the courage to do—and he reveled in every second of it. For years he had been abused by this man, this horrible creature, who had beaten him like his play thing. Now, finally, he had vengeance. After all those years, all those abuses.

"This is what you get for beating me," Steffen said. "Do you think you're the only one with power here? How do you like it now?"

His master hissed and gasped, and finally collapsed into a heap on the floor.

Dead.

Steffen looked at him, lying there, just the two of them down here this late in the night, the dagger protruding from his heart. Steffen looked both ways, satisfied the room was empty, then extracted the dagger and wrapped it back in its rag, and stashed it back in its hiding place, behind the brick. There was something about that blade, some evil energy to it, that had goaded him to use it.

As Steffen stood there, looking at the corpse of his master, he was suddenly overwhelmed with panic. What had he done? He had never done anything like that in his life. He did not know what had overcome him.

He bent over, hoisted his master's corpse, heaved it over his shoulder, then leaned forward and dropped it into the chamber pot. The body landed with a splash, as the filthy water spilled over its sides. Luckily the pot was deep, and his corpse sank beneath the rim.

On the next shift, Steffen would carry the pot out with his friend, a man so down and drunk, he never had any idea what was in the pot, a man who always turned away from it, holding his nose from the stench. He wouldn't even realize that the pot was heavier than usual as the two of them carried it to the river and dumped it. He wouldn't even notice the mass in the night, the body floating away, down the current.

Down, Steffen hoped, towards hell.

CHAPTER FIFTEEN

Gareth sat on his father's throne, in the vast council chamber, in the midst of his first council meeting, and inwardly, he trembled. Before him, in the imposing room, seated around the semi-circular table, sat a dozen of his father's counselors, all seasoned veterans, all staring back at him with gravity and doubt. Gareth was in over his head. The reality of it all was starting to sink in. This was his father's throne. His father's room. His father's affairs. And above all, his father's men. Each and every one of them loyal to his father. Gareth secretly wondered if they all suspected him of having murdered him. He told himself he was just being paranoid. But he felt increasingly uncomfortable, staring back at them.

Gareth also, for the first time, felt the real weight of what it was like to rule. All the burdens, all the decisions, all the responsibilities, were on his head. He felt woefully unprepared. Being king was what he'd always dreamed of. But ruling the kingdom, on a daily, practical level, was something he had not.

The council had been going over various matters with him for hours, and he'd had no idea of how to decide on each one. He could not help but feel as if each new matter was raised secretly as a rebuke to him, as a way to foil him, to highlight his lack of knowledge. He realized too quickly that he did not have the acumen or judgment of his father, or the experience to rule this kingdom. He was woefully unqualified to be making these decisions. And he knew, even as he made them, that all of his decisions were bad ones.

Above all, he found it hard to focus, knowing the investigation was still ongoing into his father's murder. He could not help but wonder if, or when, it might lead back to him—or to Firth, which was as good as leading to him. He could not rest easy on the throne until he knew he held it securely. He prepared to set into motion a plan to frame someone else. It was risky. But then again, so was murdering his father.

"My Liege," another council member said, each one looking more grave than the next. It was Owen, his father's treasurer, and he looked down at the table as he spoke, squinting at a long scroll. The more he unrolled it, the longer it seemed to get.

"I'm afraid our treasury is near bankrupt. The situation is grave. I warned your father of this, but he did not take action. He did not want to raise a new tax on the people, or the Lords. Frankly, he did not have a plan. I presume he thought that somehow it would all work out. But it has not. The army needs to be fed. Weapons need to be repaired. Blacksmiths need to be paid. Horses need to be tended, and fed. And yet our treasury's nearly empty. What do you propose we do, my lord?"

Gareth sat there, his mind swimming, wondering what to do. He had absolutely no idea.

"What would *you* propose?" Gareth asked back.

Owen cleared his throat, looking flustered. It seemed as if this were the first time a king had asked him his opinion.

"Well…my liege…I…um… I had proposed to your father that we raise a tax on the people. But he had thought it a bad idea."

"It *is* a bad idea," Earnan chimed in. "The people will revolt with any new taxes. And without the power of the people, you have nothing."

Gareth turned and looked at the teenage boy seated to his right, not far from him. Berel, a friend of his, who he had grown up with, someone his own age; he was an aristocrat with no military training, but who was as ambitious and cynical as he. Gareth had brought in a small group of his own advisers, his friends, to help balance out the power here, and to have some advisers his own age. A new generation. It had not gone over well when they had arrived with Gareth, upsetting the old guard.

"And what do you think, Berel?" he asked.

Berel leaned forward, arching an eyebrow, and without pausing, said, in his deep, confident voice: "Tax them. Tax them triple. Make the people feel the yoke of your new power. Make them fear you. That is the only way to rule."

"And how would you know what it means to rule?" Aberthol called out to Berel.

"Excuse me my liege, but who is this person?" Brom called out, equally indignant. "We are the

King's Council. And we never sanctioned any new councilmen."

"The Council is mine to do with as I wish," Gareth chided back. "This is one of my new advisers. Berel. And I like his idea. We will tax the people triple. We will fill our coffers, and even more, we will make the people suffer under the burden of it. Then they will understand that I am King. And that I am to be feared—even more so than my father."

Aberthol shook he said.

"My Liege, I would caution against such a harsh response. Everything in moderation. Such a move is rash. You will alienate your subjects."

"*My* subjects," Gareth spat. "That is exactly what they are. And I will do with them as I wish. This matter is ended. What other matters are before me?"

The council members turned to each other and exchanged troubled glances.

Suddenly, Brom rose.

"My Liege, with all respect, I cannot sit on a council that does heed our advice. I sat on this council for years for your father, and I am here to serve you out of deference to him. But you are not my King. He was. And I shall not serve on any council that does not pay homage and respect to its original councilmembers. You have brought in these young outsiders who know nothing of ruling a kingdom. I will not be a part of this facade. I hereby resign from this council."

Brom scraped back his chair, got up and marched from the room, yanking open the door and slamming it behind him. The hollow sound echoed in the chamber, reverberating again and again.

Inwardly, Gareth's heart was pounding. He felt the deck of cards crumbling around him. Had he gone too far?

"Never mind," Gareth said. "We do not need him. I will bring in my own adviser on military affairs."

"Do not need him, my Lord?" Aberthol echoed. "He is our greatest general, and was your father's best adviser."

"My father's advisers are not *my* advisers," Gareth threatened. "It is a new era. Is there anyone else here unhappy with this arrangement? If so, you can leave now."

Gareth's heart pounded as he sat there expecting the others to walk out, too.

To his surprise, none did. They all looked frozen in shock. He felt he had to assert his authority, had to make this kingdom his own.

Sweating now, Gareth just wanted this meeting, which had already gone on for hours, over with.

"Any other news, or can we finish?" he asked, peremptorily.

"My Liege, there is another important matter," Bradaigh said. "News of your father's death has spread to all corners of the Ring, and has reached the McClouds. Our spies inform us that they are meeting with a contingent from the Wilds. The rumor is that they intend to attack, either alone or with the Empire in tow. They may allow them to breach the Eastern Crossing of the Canyon. I suggest we mobilize our forces, and double our patrols of the Highlands."

Gareth sat there, rooted in place, unsure what to do. He had never had any skill when it came to military affairs, and the thought of the McClouds invading terrified him.

"The McClouds will not let the Empire breach the Canyon," he said. "That would imperil them, too. They might attack, though, even with my sister as their new Princess. Maybe we should not wait. Maybe we should attack them first."

"Attack them unprovoked?" Kelvin asked. "And spark an all-out war?"

Gareth considered the possibilities, resting his hand on his chin, wondering when this would all be over. He wanted to be outside; he did not want to think any more of these affairs. And he wanted to get off his mind his most pressing concern—the investigation into his father's murder.

"I will consider what to do," Gareth said curtly. "In the meantime, I must raise a much more pressing matter, concerning the murder of my father. It has been brought to my attention that the assassin has been found."

"What!?"

"What my Lord?"

"Who? How?!"

The councilmembers all yelled out at once, some of them standing in shock and outrage.

Gareth smiled inwardly, realizing he had them exactly where he wanted them. He turned and nodded towards Firth, who, standing on the outskirts of the room, walked across it, holding something small in his palm. Firth made a show of reaching out and handing it to Gareth, and as he did, Gareth held it up so that the others could see. He leaned forward on his throne and held out the small vial.

"Sheldrake Root. The same root used in the first attempt to poison my father at that night's feast. As you can see, this vial is nearly empty. This vial was found in the killer's chamber, on that very night."

"But who is the killer, my Lord?" Aberthol yelled out.

"It pains me to say," Gareth pronounced slowly, doing his best to feign sadness, "that it is my eldest brother. My Lord's firstborn son. Kendrick."

"What!"

"An outrage!"

"It can't be!" they yelled back.

"Oh, I'm afraid it is," Gareth replied. "We have gathered ample evidence. As we speak, I'm sending our men to arrest him. He will be imprisoned and tried for the death of my father."

The council broke out in outraged mumbling.

"But Kendrick was the most loved of your father!" Duwayne yelled out. "And the most loyal of all."

"It must be a mistake," Bradaigh yelled.

"And our own committee is still investigating the matter!" Kelvin shouted.

"You can call off the investigation," Gareth responded. "It is concluded."

"It makes perfect sense," Firth said, stepping forward. "He has a motive. Kendrick was the firstborn son. He was passed over. He must have had a vendetta, and must have pined for the throne himself."

The councilmen turned and exchanged troubled, skeptical glances.

"You are wrong," Aberthol said. "Kendrick is not ambitious. He is a loyal warrior."

The councilmen debated with each other, and as Gareth watched them, he smiled inwardly. This was exactly what he'd wanted: to plant doubt in their minds. He had achieved his vision. He had found a scapegoat, planted evidence, and gave himself cover to imprison him. He would not give him a trial. He would let the kingdom know that the matter had been settled, quickly and easily. And in the process, he would remove one more threat from the crown.

Gareth sat back, satisfied with himself, and watched and enjoyed the chaos spreading before him. He was beginning to realize that it suited him, after all, being King.

It suited him very well.

CHAPTER SIXTEEN

Thor marched amidst the huge contingent of Legion members, Krohn at his heels, Reese, O'Connor, Elden and the twins at his side, all of them heading down a wide, dirt road which never seemed to end. They had been marching for hours, heading towards the distant Canyon, preparing for their first leg of the journey to the Tartuvian Sea. Thor had made it back in time from his night with Gwen, had awakened with the dawn and arrived first thing in the morning at the barracks; he'd joined the others as they were rising, prepared all his things, grabbed his sack, his sling, his weapons, and left with the others just in time.

Thor could hardly believe he was embarking on this journey with all these boys, on his way to what he knew would be the most challenging hundred days of his life—on his way to leaving boyhood behind and becoming a man. His heart pounded with anticipation. He could feel the excited buzz in the air, and also the tension. Some boys walked with a bounce in their step, but others kept silent, and wore scared expressions. When Thor had arrived, he heard reports that two Legion members had fled during the night, apparently too scared to embark on The Hundred. He was glad that none of his newfound friends had left.

Thor might have been flooded with anxiety, too, but, luckily, he was also preoccupied, his mind swimming with other things. Gwendolyn. His night with her lingered over him like a cloud; he could not shake the image of her face, the sound of her voice, her energy. It was as if she were with him right now. It had been a magical day and night, the best of his entire life. His heart soared as he thought of her; knowing that she existed made him feel as if everything would be all right in the world, no matter what happened during the Hundred. As long as he had her, he had reason to survive, and reason to return. He felt that would carry him through.

They had mourned together for her father, and having her at his side had brought him a sense of peace and solace he hadn't had before; being able to share it with her had somehow made it all the more bearable. It had also made them closer. He closed his eyes and saw that lake she had taken him to, its white and blue waters, that island, so secluded from the world; it was the most magical place he had ever been. He remembered their looking up at the stars, all night long, she lying in his arms. She had slept like that, in his arms, all night long. Neither of them had taken off their clothes, but they had kissed all night, and she had finally curled up in a ball, and lay her head on his chest. It was the first time a girl had slept in his arms. At some points during the night she had cried, and he knew she was thinking of her father.

He had awakened at the first light of dawn, a beautiful red light blanketing the horizon with the first rising sun, and all had felt right in the world. He had awakened with her still in his arms, the feel of her on his chest, the warmth of her, the complete perfect stillness of the summer morning; there was a light breeze, the trees swaying above him, and all had felt perfect in the world. It was the first time he'd ever awakened feeling a true sense of comfort, of belonging, of love. For the first time, he felt *wanted* by somebody, and that meant more to him than he could say.

They had parted ways sadly early in the morning, Thor needing to rush back to the Legion before they left. She had cried quietly, tears dripping down her cheek, and had leaned in and hugged him—and would not let go for a long time.

"Vow to me again," she had whispered, "that you will return."

"I vow," he'd said.

He could still remember the look in her teary eyes as she looked back at him in the early morning light, filled with such hope and longing. That look sustained him now. Even now he saw those eyes, as he walked on this road with all of his Legion brothers.

"I'm not looking forward to crossing the Canyon again," came a voice.

Thor snapped out of it, looked over, and saw Elden, a few feet away, anxiety on his face. In the distance was the outline of the bridge. The Eastern Crossing of the Canyon. Hundreds of soldiers were lined up along it.

"Nor I," O'Connor added.

"It will be different this time," Reese said. "We go as a group. We are in the Wilds only for a short bit, and then we are at the ships. Is a direct route to the ships. We do not venture deep into their territory before we hit the ocean."

"Still, we're beyond the Canyon, and anything could happen," Conval said.

The group fell silent, and Thor listened to the sound of hundreds of boots crushing rocks, of Krohn panting beside him, of horses, being walked next to some of the warriors, clomping; he could smell the horses from here, the sweat of men afraid. Thor was not afraid. He was excited. Nervous, maybe. And overwhelmed with longing for Gwendolyn.

"Just think, when we return, next season, we will all be different men," O'Connor said. "None of us will be the same."

"*If* we return," Reese corrected.

Thor took a good look at all the boys and men around him, and he thought about that. Nothing would ever be the same. He felt the world constantly changing around him, every minute of every day; it was so hard to hold onto anything. He wanted to freeze all of this, but even as he did, he knew that he could not.

*

They finally reached the base of the Western Crossing of the Canyon, and the group of them paused before stepping onto the bridge. Thor could see the look of wonder and fear in the eyes of his fellow Legion members. He remembered when he had first seen it, and he understood how they felt. Even now, looking at it for his second time, it inspired the same sense of awe and fear and wonder in him: the bridge spanned forever, disappearing from site, and the drop-off below was bottomless. Although the bridge was lined with hundreds of the King's soldiers, it felt as if the first step onto the bridge was a step of no return.

They all proceeded onto the bridge, marching silently forward, and as they did, Thor felt the stakes raised. No longer was this another training exercise; now they were leaving the actual protection of the Ring. Now they would be real warriors, out there in the Wilds, where anyone could kill them at any moment. Now, it was life or death.

Everybody came a little bit closer to each other as they marched, and Thor could see the others clenching up, tightening their hands on their swords, everybody more on edge. Howling winds whipped at them from every direction, and more than one of them looked over the edge, then quickly pulled back. Despite himself, Thor looked, too, and immediately wished he hadn't: he saw a plunge down to nothingness, ending in a mist. He swallowed hard, and wondered for the millionth time about the power of this place. Krohn whined, and came in close to Thor, rubbing against his ankles.

They marched and marched, and the span over the Canyon felt like it would last forever.

Thor heard a distant screech, and looked up to see Ephistopheles, high up, circling. She dove down, lower and lower, until finally she dove down right for Thor. Thor lowered his canvas sleeve and raised one arm, hoping that she would land on it. But instead she dove right at him, and as she got close, he could see she was carrying something in her claw. It looked like a scroll. As she neared, she opened her talons and let it drop; it flew through the air, landing near Thor's feet. She screeched, flapped her wings, and flew off again.

Krohn ran over to it, picked it up in his mouth and brought it to Thor. Thor bent down, curious, and took the piece of parchment.

"What is it?" Reese asked.

"A message, perhaps?" O'Connor remarked.

Thor held it close as he opened it, slowly unrolling it, feeling protective of whatever it was. Clearly, it was a message just for him. Before he'd even finished unrolling it, he spotted the handwriting, and knew who it was from. He held it even closer, guarding it jealously. It was from Gwen.

He read with trembling hands as he walked:

Many days will pass until we see each other again. It is possible we may not see each other at all. I cannot begin to tell you how this makes me feel. I cannot stop thinking of you. I'm with you, on your journeys, wherever it is you go. Know that you hold my heart in your hands. Do not hold it lightly. Think of me. And return to me.

Yours in love,

Gwendolyn

"What is it?" Elden asked.

"What message do you hold?" Conval prodded.

But Thor rolled up the scroll and tucked it away in his pocket, not sure that he wanted the others to know.

"Is it from my sister?" Reese asked softly.

Thor waited until the others were not watching, then nodded back.

Reese nodded, then turned back to the road.

"She has fallen for you, my friend. I hope that you treat her well. She is delicate. And I care for her very much."

Thor's heart beat faster as he read her message again in his mind. It was strange, because he had been thinking of little else but her, and to receive an actual message from her, dropped down from the sky, made his thoughts seem to manifest into reality. He loved her more than he could say, and in a sense, he was already counting the days until his return. For the first time in a long time, he felt he had something strong to hold onto.

Thor did not know how much time had passed when they finally stepped off the bridge and stepped onto the soil on the far side of the Canyon. But he felt it like an electric jolt, felt the leaving of the Ring, beyond the protection of the energy shield. He immediately felt unprotected.

The others must have felt it too, because he could see them all tense up, hands on their weapons, as they looked all about them in wonder. Strange animal noises rose up as they followed the path as one, into a deep and dark wood.

Kolk stepped forward and faced the group.

"You'll stay together, close as a group, your weapons drawn. We will move as one through this wood. It will be many miles until we hit the ocean. Our ships are waiting and ready to board, our men guarding them. The Empire's army is camped too far to cause any trouble. But there could be isolated attackers. Stay alert."

One hour after another passed as the path narrowed, the sky darkened, and they marched deeper into the twisting trails of the dark wood. Foreign animal noises persisted all around them, and Thor felt always on guard. There came occasional scrambling in the branches, and he and his brothers flinched more than once, but nothing ever attacked them.

Hours more passed, and finally the wood broke open: in the distance Thor could see, with great relief, and with a sense of awe, the crashing waves of the Tartuvian Sea. He heard them from here, and could already feel the change in the air. There was a wide open plain between here and there, and no sign of the enemy as far as he could see. He breathed a sigh of relief.

A huge, wooden ship sat there, sails fluttering high in the air, waiting for them, surrounded by the King's Men, standing guard.

"We made it!" O'Connor said.

"No we didn't," Elden said. "We reached the ships, that is all. We still have to cross the ocean. That will be much worse."

"I hear that the island is many days' sail away," Conval said. "The waves of the Tartuvian are supposedly stronger than a man can stand, its weather awful, and the sea filled with monsters and hostile ships. Our journey has not yet even begun."

Thor looked at the ships, standing proud on the horizon, their sails gleaming white as the second sun broke free from the clouds, and he felt the thrill of excitement. Already, the Ring was behind them.

CHAPTER SEVENTEEN

Erec sat at the table of honor in the large banquet hall, filled with hundreds of guests of the Duke. He had not expected his arrival here to cause such fanfare, and was a bit overwhelmed by all the attention. He knew he was an important person in the kingdom, especially because of his relationship with the King, but he had not anticipated the extent to which the Duke would roll out the red carpet for him. It was their second day of feasting in celebration of Erec's arrival and in anticipation of the tournament to come. Erec was stuffed with good food and wine. He knew that if he didn't compete soon, his skills might not be as sharp.

As Erec leaned back on the deep cushions and looked around, he observed knights from all corners of the Ring, all dressed in different-colored attire, speaking with different accents, using different mannerisms. They all looked like formidable warriors, and while the Duke was confident Erec would beat them all, Erec took nothing for granted. It was part of his training. While the servants re-filled his goblet with wine, he only sipped at it. The tournament was tomorrow, and he wanted to be in a good space. After all, he felt that his actions, and his performance, reflected on the King. And that was something he took very seriously.

Whether he would find a bride here was a different matter entirely. He smiled to himself at the thought of it. The last two days, it seemed that every fine woman in the kingdom had been introduced to him. Indeed, as he looked about the room, he saw dozens of beautiful women seated throughout, and could not help but notice that most of them looked his way. He seemed to also draw the jealousy of the other men in the room, who competed for their attention. But Erec himself did not feel jealous or competitive. He had been introduced to all of them, and had been impressed by them all, each more beautiful, more fine mannered, dressed more elaborately, than the next. He felt honored to have met them all, but he had decided long ago to choose his bride based on his gut instinct. And for whatever mysterious reason, he had not felt that certain feeling when meeting any of them. He did not mean to be picky. He felt certain that these women would all be great for someone; he just did not feel that they were right for him.

"Erec of the Southern Island Province of the Ring, may I introduce to you Dessbar, of the Second Province of the Lowlands," the Duke said to Erec, as he turned to meet yet another fair maiden. The parade of introductions seemed to never end. This one was beautiful, too, dressed in white silk from head to toe, and she curtsied and smiled a gracious smile.

"It is a pleasure, my Lord."

"The pleasure is mine," Erec said, standing out of courtesy and kissing her fingertips.

"Dessbar comes from Emerald Plains, and from a noble family of the East. Her mother is third cousin to the Queen. She is of noble blood. She would make a fine match," the Duke said.

Erec nodded graciously, not wanting to offend her, or the Duke.

"I can tell that she is of a fine lineage," Erec said with a short bow. "It is a great privilege to meet you."

With that, he kissed her hand again, and seated himself. She looked somewhat disappointed, as if she wanted to talk to him more; the Duke did, too.

But Erec did not feel whatever it was he was supposed to feel when he met this woman. And he wanted to approach finding his wife with the same discipline he did battle—with a single-minded focus and intensity.

The feast went on, deep into the night, and Erec was glad to at least be in the company of his old friend, Brandt, seated on his right. They'd been sharing battle stories for half the night, and as the fires grew long and people filtered from the hall, they were still recounting stories.

"Remember that hill?" Brandt asked. "When it was just the four of us, on patrol? Up against the entire company of McClouds?"

Erec nodded. "Too well."

"I swear, if it wasn't for you, I would be dead."

Erec shook his head. "I got lucky."

"You never get lucky," Brandt said. "You're the finest knight in the kingdom."

"It is true," the Duke echoed, seated on his other side. "I fear for any knight who comes against you tomorrow."

"I'm not so sure," Erec said, humbly. "You seem to have a vast array of warriors gathered here."

"That's true, there are," the Duke said. "They've descended on us from all corners of the Ring. It seems that every man wants the same thing in this world: a fine woman. God knows why. Once we get one, we can't wait to get rid of her!"

The men all laughed.

"Tomorrow will certainly be a site," the Duke added. "But I have no doubt in you."

"The only problem is," Brandt chimed in, "is that the winner chooses a bride. Knowing you, you may choose no one—and offend every woman here!"

Erec shook his head.

"I mean no offense," he said. "I suppose…I suppose I just have not found her yet."

"Are you telling me that not a single woman here suits you?" the Duke asked, surprised. "You have met some of the finest women this court has to offer. Any man here would die for some of them—and tomorrow, some of them just might."

"I mean no offense, my lord," Erec said. "I do not consider myself more worthy than any of them. On the contrary, surely they are all more worthy than I. It is just that…well, I feel that I will know her when I see her. I don't want to be hasty."

"Hasty!" Brandt yelled. "You've had twenty five years! How much more time do you want!?"

They all laughed.

"Just make a choice," Brandt added, "and be weighed down with a bride and join the rest of our miserable lot. After all, misery loves company! And our kingdom must populate!"

The group laughed again, and as Erec looked away, somewhat embarrassed by all the talk, his eyes froze. He happened to see, across the room, a serving girl, perhaps eighteen, with long, blonde hair, and large, almond green eyes. She wore a simple servant's attire, hardly better than rags, as she went down the tables, person to person, filling vessels with wine. She kept her head down, never making eye contact, and was more humble than anyone Erec had ever seen. She was huddled with the other serving girls, and they worked hard. No one paid them any attention. They were of the servant class, and here, in court, class distinctions were treated very seriously: servants were treated as if they did not exist. Her clothes were soiled, and her hair looked as if it had not been washed in days. She looked dejected.

And yet the second Erec saw her, it was as if he had been struck by lightning. Erec sensed something exuding from her which was special. She had a proud, even a regal, quality. Something told him that she was different than the others.

As she came closer, filling each goblet, he caught a good look at her face as she turned, and his breath stopped. He had never felt this way before, not upon meeting anyone, not even any royalty. It was the feeling he had been hoping to feel his entire life. The feeling he did not know if he was ever capable of feeling.

She was magnificent. He could hardly speak. He had to know who she was.

"Who is that woman?" Erec asked the Duke, nodding.

The Duke and several others turned excitedly to follow his gaze.

"Which do you mean? Esmeralda? With the blue gown?"

"No," Erec said, pointing. "Her."

They all followed his glance in silence and confusion.

"Do you mean the servant girl?" ___ asked.

Erec nodded.

The Duke shrugged.

"Who knows? Just another servant," he said dismissively. "Why do you ask? Do you know her?"

"No," Erec answered, his voice catching in his throat. "But I wish to."

The girl came closer, and reached their group, and bent down to fill Erec's goblet. He was so mesmerized, he forgot to raise it.

Finally, she looked up at him. As she did, so close, as her eyes met his, he felt his whole world melt away.

"My Lord?" she asked, staring back at him. Her eyes froze in his, and seemed to widen, too. She, too, seemed captivated by him. It was as if they were meeting again.

"My Lord?" she repeated, after several seconds. "Shall I fill your goblet?"

Erec stared at her, forgetting his manners, too dumbfounded to speak. After several seconds of staring back at him, finally, she moved on. She turned and checked back over her shoulder a few times as she went, looking at him.

Then finally, she set down the pitcher, turned, and ran from the hall.

Erec stood, watching her.

"I must know her," Erec said to the Duke.

"*Her*?" the Duke asked, in shock.

"But she's a servant girl. Why would you want to know her?" Brandt asked.

Erec stood, electrified, knowing for the first time exactly what he wanted.

"She is the one I want. She is the one I will fight for."

"*Her*!?" Brandt asked, stunned, standing beside him.

The Duke stood, too.

"You could choose any woman in the kingdom, on both sides of the Ring. You could choose a princess. A lord's daughter. A woman with a dowry as wide as the kingdom. And you would choose her? A servant girl?"

But their words hardly phased Erec. He watched, mesmerized, as she fled from the hall, out a side room.

"Where is she going?" he demanded. "I must know."

"Erec, are you sure about this?" Brandt asked.

"You are making a grave mistake," the Duke added. "And you would snub all the women here, all of high royalty."

Erec turned to him, earnest.

"I aim to snub no one," he answered. "But that is the woman I am going to marry. Will you help me find her?"

The Duke nodded to his attendant, who ran off, on the mission.

He raised a hand and clasped Erec's shoulder, and broke into a hearty smile.

"It is true what they say about you, my friend. You do not defer to what others think. And that is, I think, what I love about you best."

The Duke sighed.

"We will find you this servant girl. And we will make a match!"

A cheer rose up around Erec, as others clasped him on his back. But he paid attention to none of it. His mind was only on one thing: that girl. He felt, without a doubt, that he had found the love of his life.

CHAPTER EIGHTEEN

Gareth stood there, in his father's ruling chamber, looking out through the open window over King's Court, like his father used to love to do. His father used to stroll out, onto the parapets, but Gareth felt no need to do that. He was perfectly happy, standing here, indoors, at the edge of the window, hands clasped loosely behind his back, and looking out over his people from the shadows.

His people. They were *his* people now. He could hardly believe it.

He stood there, rooted in place, the crown securely on his head as it had been since the ceremony. He would not take it off. He also wore his father's white and black mantle, even in the summer heat, and clutched in his hand his father's long, golden scepter. He was beginning to feel like a king—a real king—and he loved the feeling. All his subjects, as he walked, bowed to him. To *him*, not to his father. It made him feel a rush of adrenaline unlike any he had felt before. All eyes were turned to him, all hours of the day.

He had really done it. He had managed to kill his father, to cover up the crime, and to wipe out all obstacles between him and the kingship. They had all fell for it. And now that they had crowned him, there was no turning back. Now there was nothing they could do to change it.

Yet now that Gareth was King, he scarcely knew what to do. All his life he had dreamt of this moment; now that he'd achieved it, he did not know what was next. His first impression was that being king was lonely. He had stood here, alone in this room for hours, watching the court. Down below, in the lower chambers, his counsel awaited him for a meeting. He had decided to make them wait. In fact, he enjoyed making them wait. He was King, and he could make anyone wait that he wanted to, for as long as he wanted.

As he had stood here, watching over his people, he had pondered how to solidify and secure his power. To start with, he would have Kendrick imprisoned, then, executed. It was too much of a risk to have Kendrick alive, the firstborn, the most loved of his family. He smiled as he thought of the guards already on their way to take Kendrick in.

Then he would have Thor killed. He, too, was a threat, given how close he had been to his father; who knew what his father had told him while on his deathbed? Perhaps he had even identified Firth. Gareth was pleased with himself for setting into motions plans for his assassination; he had wisely paid off a Legion member to do the trick. Once they reached the Isle of Mist, he would ambush Thor and finish him off. He was assured that Thor would not return.

When Thor and Kendrick were out of the way, he would turn to Gwendolyn. She, too, posed a threat. After all, his father's last wish was for her to rule. As long as she was alive, the possibility of revolt lingered.

Finally, most importantly, was the one issue that loomed on his mind most: the Dynasty Sword. Would he attempt to wield it? If he could, it would set him apart from every MacGil king that had ever ruled. It would make all the people love him, for all time. It would mean that *he* was the chosen one, the one destined to rule. It would validate him, and it would secure his throne forever. Gareth had dreamt his whole life of the moment when he would wield it, from the time he was a boy. A part of him felt certain that he could.

Yet another part of him was not so sure.

The door to his chamber suddenly barged open, and Gareth turned, wondering who could be so impudent as to barge in on the king. His face fell as he saw that it was Firth, strutting in past the guards, who gave Gareth a befuddled look. Firth had grown too brazen since Gareth had become crowned—he acted as if he ruled the kingdom with him. Gareth resented him barging in like this, and wondered if he had made a mistake in elevating him, in making him his adviser. Yet at the same time, he had to admit that he was happy to see him. A part of him was tired of being alone. And he hardly knew who he could be friends with, now that he was King. He seemed to have isolated everyone in his life.

Gareth nodded to the guards, who closed the door behind Firth. Firth crossed the room, and embraced Gareth. He leaned back and tried to kiss him, but Gareth turned away.

Gareth wasn't in the mood for him. He'd interrupted his thoughts.

Firth looked hurt, but then quickly smiled.

"My Liege," he said, stretching out the word. "Don't you love being called that? It's so becoming of you!" Firth clapped his hands in delight. "Can you believe it? You are King. Thousands of subjects stand waiting for your every beck and call. There is nothing we cannot do!"

"*We*?" Gareth asked, darkly.

Firth hesitated.

"I mean…you, my lord. Can you imagine? Anything you want. Right now, everyone awaits your decision."

"Decision?"

"About the sword," Firth said. "The whole kingdom is whispering. That's all they're talking about. Will you attempt to wield it?"

Gareth studied him. Firth was more perceptive than he thought; maybe it was good having him as an adviser.

"And what would you suggest I do?"

"You *have* to do it! If you don't, you will be perceived as too weak to even try. They will assume that means you are not meant to be king. Because, in their eyes, if you truly felt entitled, then you would certainly try to hoist it."

Gareth thought about that. There was some truth to his words. Maybe he was right.

"Besides," Firth said, smiling, coming up beside him, linking arms and walking with him towards the window. "You *are* meant to be king. You are the one."

Gareth turned and looked at him, already feeling aged.

"No I'm not," he said, honestly. "I took the throne. It was not handed to me."

"That does not mean you're not meant to have it," Firth said. "We are only given what we are meant to have in this life. For some, destiny is handed to them; others need to take it for themselves. That makes you greater, my lord, not lesser. Think about it," he said, "you're the only MacGil to have taken a throne, who didn't sit back and have it lazily handed to him. Does that mean something to you? It does to me. To me, it means that you, and you alone of all the MacGils are the one meant to wield the sword, to rule forever. And if you do, just imagine: all the peoples, from all corners of the Ring and beyond will bow down to you, forever. You will unite the Ring. No one would ever doubt your legitimacy."

Firth turned and looked at him, his eyes shining with excitement and anticipation.

"You have to try!"

Gareth pulled away from Firth, crossing the room. He thought about it, wanting to take it all in. Firth had a point. Maybe he *was* destined to be king. Maybe he had underestimated himself; maybe he had just been too hard on himself. After all, his father was meant to die—or else he would not have died. Maybe it all happened this way because Gareth was meant to be the better king. Yes, maybe his killing his father was for the *good* of the kingdom.

Gareth heard a shout, and he turned and looked out over King's Court and saw the parade passing below, the celebration for the new King, the banners being hoisted. He saw his soldiers marching in formation. It was a beautiful, perfect summer day. As he looked down, he could not help feeling as if all of this had been destined. Like Firth said: if he was not meant to be king, he would not be king. He would not be standing here right now.

He knew this was the most important decision of his entire kingship, and it was one he would have to make now. He wished that Argon were here now, to offer him counsel, but he also sensed that Argon hated him, and even if he gave him advice, he wondered if it would be the right advice.

Gareth sighed, then finally turned from the window. The time had come to make the first major decision of his kingship.

"Summon the guards," he ordered Firth, as he turned and walked for the door. "Prepare the dynasty chamber."

He stopped and turned to Firth, who stood there, staring back excitedly.

"I am going to wield the sword."

CHAPTER NINETEEN

King McCloud sat on his horse on the peak of the Highlands, flanked by his son, his top generals, and hundreds of his men, as he looked down greedily at the MacGil's side of the Ring. On this summer day a warm breeze pushed back his long hair, and he peered down at their lush land with envy. It was the land he'd always wished for, the land his father and his father before him had always wanted, the choicer side of the Ring, with more fertile land, deeper rivers, richer soil, and purer water. His side of the Highlands, the McCloud side of the Ring, had been adequate, maybe even good. But it wasn't choice. It wasn't the MacGil side. He didn't have the very best vineyards, the richest milk, the brightest rays of the sun. And McCloud, as his father before him, was determined to change that. The MacGils had enjoyed the better half of the Ring for long enough; now it was time for the McClouds to have it.

As McCloud sat at the very top of the Highlands, eyeing the MacGil side for the first time since he was a boy, he felt optimism. The fact that he was even able to be up this high told him everything he needed to know. In the past, the MacGils had always guarded the Highlands so carefully that the McClouds could not even find a single way to pass through—and certainly could not sit on the high ground. Now his men had cleared it with only the slightest skirmish. The MacGils were truly not expecting an attack from their ancient adversaries. It was either that or, McCloud supposed, the new MacGil king was weak, unprepared. Gareth. He'd met him on several occasions. He was nothing like his father. To think that the kingdom was now in his hands was laughable.

McCloud knew an opportunity when he saw it—and this one was once in a lifetime, one that could not be passed by. It was a chance to strike the MacGils hard, once and for all, deep in their territory, before they had had a chance to reconvene from the death of the king. McCloud was gambling that they would still be reeling, still unsure how to react under the rule of this novice king. Thus far, he had been right.

McCloud speculated even further, reasoned that MacGil's assassination pointed to a division within the MacGil dynasty. Someone had executed him, and had gone about it very well. There were chinks in the armor, all down the chain. That meant weakness. Division. All excellent signs. All pointing to a fractured kingdom. All pointing to the McClouds, after centuries, finally having their chance to crush them once and for all, and to control the entire Ring.

McCloud smiled at the thought of it, as close to a smile as he could come, the slightest bit at the corner of his mouth, barely moving his thick, stiff beard. All around him, he could feel his men watching him as he watched the horizon, looking to him for the first sign of what to do, how to act. What he saw below pleased him immensely. There were small villages, spread out in bucolic hills, smoke rising from chimneys, women hanging clothes out to dry, children playing. There were entire fields of sheep, farmers harvesting fruits—and most importantly, no patrols in sight. The MacGils had become sloppy.

His smile broadened. Soon, those would be *his* women. Soon, those would be *his* sheep.

"ATTACK!" McCloud shrieked.

His men let out a cheer, a battle cry, all of them on horses, raising their swords high.

As one, they all charged, hundreds of them, down the mountain. McCloud went first, as he always did, the wind in his hair, his stomach dropping as he stormed down the steep descent. And as he kicked his horse mercilessly, galloping faster, ever faster, he had never felt so alive.

CHAPTER TWENTY

Kendrick sat in the Hall of Arms on a long, wooden bench, seated beside dozens of his brothers in arms, members of The Silver. He studied his sword as he sharpened it. His spirits were broken. His father's passing had hurt him more than he could say. As long as he had lived, the way that the word perceived his relationship with his father had troubled him. MacGil was his true father. He knew that, deep in his heart. He treated him like a true father, and he knew that to MacGil he was a true son. His true firstborn son. Yet for the eyes of all the world, he was illegitimate. Why? Only because his father chose another woman to be his queen.

It was unfair. He had accepted his role as bastard and had played the good son out of respect for his father. He had dutifully repressed his feelings his entire life. But now that his father was dead, and especially now that Gareth was named King, something within Kendrick could no longer accept the status quo. Something inside him fumed. It was not that he wanted to be king; it was just that he wanted the rest of the world to acknowledge that he was MacGil's first born, that he was legitimate—as much as any of his half-siblings.

As MacGil sat there, sharpening his sword with the stone, again and again, making a high-pitched noise that cut through the room, he thought about all the things left unsaid to his father. He wished he had more time, wished he'd had a chance to tell him how grateful he was for raising him as one of his own. To tell him that no matter what the world thought, he was his true father, and he his true son. To tell him the words he had never spoken: that he loved him.

His father had been taken away from him too soon, and without warning.

Kendrick sharpened the sword harder, digging the stone into it, as rage rose up within him. He would find his father's murderer. And he would kill him himself. He was determined. Many suspects floated in his head, and hour to hour he pondered one after the next. The one he pondered most of all, unfortunately, was the one he was most afraid to think of. The one closest to him. His younger half-brother, Gareth.

Deep down he could not help but wonder if Gareth was behind it somehow. He remembered that meeting, Gareth's rage at being skipped over for Gwendolyn. Raised with him, only a few years apart, he knew, too well, Gareth's devious nature; as long as he had known him, Gareth had envied Kendrick, being older, being firstborn. He had viewed Kendrick as an obstacle. He felt that Gareth would stop at nothing to have the kingship.

Kendrick sharpened the sword as he pondered other suspects; there were many enemies his father had accumulated, enemies of the state, enemies he had conquered in battle; rival lords. These hit less close to home and were easier to dwell on. He hoped it was one of them. And he would explore each one. But no matter how hard he tried to think of others, again and again he found himself returning to his half-brother.

Kendrick sat back and looked around at the other Silver, all maintaining their weapons on this dreary day. The summer sun had been replaced by sudden fog and showers. The day after the summer solstice always brought great change, was always considered a day of maintenance, in preparation for the new season. It was also the day the Legion left for The Hundred. Kendrick recalled his new squire, Thor, leaving, and he smiled; he had taken a liking to the boy, and expected great things of him.

As Kendrick studied the other members of the Silver, many of them older, hardened warriors, all sitting around the table, joking with each other, all with formidable weapons, he felt grateful, as always, to be a member of their ranks. They had accepted him as a true member—and he had earned it. At first, when he was younger, he had been greeted warily; many assumed he was only here because of his father, or that he, being royalty, would look down on them. But slowly, over time, he had earned their respect; he had fought his way up, side by side with them at the hardest battles, and they had come to see he was like them. Eventually, they had accepted him as one of their own. He took great pride in that. Whenever anyone had tried to show him favor for being the King's son, he had always insisted on being treated as one of the common men. Over time, the men had come to see that he was genuine, and they had come to love him. Over many years, Kendrick knew that he had become the most loved member of the royal family—even more so than his father. He was the only one, in fact, that the Silver respected and treated as a true soldier, in his own right.

That meant more to Kendrick than anything he had done in this world. All he'd ever wanted was to be a true and respected warrior of the Silver. Looking around, he saw the respect in his brothers in arms' eyes, and could tell that many of them, especially the younger ones, were beginning to look to him as a leader. Since the death of his father, more than one of them had come up to him and expressed dismay that he had not been chosen to be king. He could feel they wanted him as their leader. But his father clearly had wanted Gwen to rule, and above all, Kendrick felt he must honor his father's wishes. That was what mattered most to him.

On the other hand, he resented Gareth's usurping the throne and worried for the future of the kingdom. Gwen was not strong enough to lead a revolt of the men. If it came down to it, then he would rather rule over Gareth, only for the sake of the well-being of the Ring. When Gwen was older and able, he would gladly hand power to her.

"What did you think of the ceremony?" asked Atme, sitting beside him, oiling down his axe handle. Atme was a fierce knight with bright-red hair and beard, from the far Eastern corner of the kingdom; Kendrick had fought with him in too many battles. He was a close and trusted friend.

"What do you think of your younger brother's being king?" he added.

Kendrick looked back at him, saw his earnest expression, and saw behind him several more members of the Silver, watching for his response. He could see in their eyes how badly they all wanted him to be King—and how anxious they were for his brother's rule. No one trusted his brother. That much was obvious.

Kendrick debated how to respond, how much to say. It was clear from Atme's use of the term "younger" that he was goading him on. What he wanted to answer was: *I think it is horribly unfair. Gareth is unfit to rule. It is a disaster. He will bring our kingdom to its knees. My father never wished for this. He is turning over in his grave, and something must be done.*

But he could not say this. Not to these men. Not now. He would demoralize them, and possibly cause a revolt. He had to think carefully of his next move, of how best to handle the situation. In the meantime, he had to be careful with his words.

"Time will tell the fate of all things," he answered, noncommittal.

The men turned and looked away, nodding, pretending to be satisfied. But he knew that they were not.

Suddenly, a great crash came through the doors of the hall, and all heads turned as in rushed a dozen of the King's Guard. Kendrick was surprised that they would burst in like this, into the hall of The Silver, and that they would dare bear arms inside this hall. It was something he had never seen before.

The Silver, hardened warriors, all reacted, wheeling, watching.

The King's Guard rushed through the room, a dozen of them, and as Kendrick watched, they headed right for him. They wore stern expressions, and Kendrick wondered what was going on. He could detect their urgency and at first wondered if they were coming here with a request for help.

They stopped before him and one of them, one of his father's deputies, Darloc, a man who Kendrick recognized and who had been loyal to his father for years, stepped forward with a grim expression.

"Kendrick of the Clan MacGil of the Western Kingdom of the Ring," he announced in a formal, grave voice, as he read from a scroll, "I hereby declare that, under law of the King, you are hereby arrested as a traitor to the realm for the assassination of King MacGil."

Kendrick's hair stood on end, and his entire body went cold.

An outraged gasp spread throughout the room, as his brothers in arms slowly stood from their seats, tense, on edge. A thick silence blanketed the room as everyone watched Kendrick for his reaction.

Kendrick stood slowly, trying to breathe, to understand. He felt as if his life flashed before him in a single moment.

Kendrick studied Darloc's face, lined and grim, and he could see that he was earnest.

"Darloc," Kendrick said steadily, forcing himself to keep calm, his voice resonating in the dead-silent room, "you have known me my entire life. You know that these words you read are not true."

Darloc's eye twitched.

"My liege," Darloc answered sadly. "I'm afraid that my personal beliefs do not matter. I am but a servant of the King and I am merely carrying out what I have been commanded to. Please forgive me. You are right. I could never believe such slander myself. But my beliefs are subservient to those of the King. I'm afraid I must follow orders."

Kendrick stared back at the man, and he could see the solemnity on his face, could see how upset, how conflicted, he was at having to be in this position. He actually felt bad for him.

Kendrick could hardly conceive the audacity of it: his own brother, accusing him of murdering their father. That could only mean one thing: Gareth was threatened, and had something to hide. He needed a scapegoat immediately, no matter how flimsy. In Kendrick's mind, that solidified it: Gareth killed him. It made a fresh fire burn within Kendrick—not because he cared about being imprisoned himself, but because he realized that Gareth was the assassin, and he felt compelled to bring him to justice.

"I am sorry, Kendrick, but I am going to have to take you in," Darloc said, and motioned to one of his men.

As the soldier took a step forward, Atme suddenly jumped to his feet and stepped like lightning between the man and Kendrick, drawing his sword.

"If you wish to touch Kendrick, you will have to go through me," came his grave voice.

Suddenly the room was filled with the sounds of swords being drawn, as every member of The Silver, dozens of them, leapt to their feet and confronted the king's guard.

Darloc stood there, looking very afraid, and in that moment he must have realized that he had very badly miscalculated coming here. He must have realized that his kingdom was just one move away a full-fledged civil war.

CHAPTER TWENTY ONE

Gwen stood on the sandy shore, as ocean waves crashed too close to her feet, huge, fierce waves, hitting her legs with enough strength to make her wobble. She stood there, losing her footing, as she watched the huge ship set sail before her, Thor standing at its helm, waving. On Thor's shoulder sat Ephistopheles, who stared back with an ominous look that made Gwen's blood run cold.

Thor was smiling, but as she watched, his sword fell from his waist and plummeted into the ocean. Oddly, he seemed not to notice, still smiling and waving, and she felt terrified for him.

The sea, so calm, suddenly turned rough, its waters turning from a crystal blue to a foaming black; as she watched, their boat was rocked violently, tossed about in the waves. Still Thor stood there, smiling and waving to her as if nothing were happening. She could not understand what was going on. Behind him the skies, clear just a moment before, turned scarlet, the clouds themselves seeming to froth over in rage. Lightning lit up the sky all around, and as she watched, a lightning bolt pierced the sail. In moments, Thor's ship was aflame. The ship, on fire, gained speed, sailed away, faster and faster, sucked out into the sea on massive currents.

"THOR!" Gwen shrieked.

She shrieked again as the ship went up into a ball of flames and was sucked into the dark red sky, disappearing on the horizon.

She looked down, and a wave crashed before her, up to her chest, knocking her onto her back. She reached out to grab hold of something—but there was nothing. She felt herself getting sucked out into the ocean, faster and faster, the currents consuming her, as another huge wave crashed down, right on her face.

Gwen shrieked.

She opened her eyes to see herself standing in her father's chamber. It was empty and freezing in here, nighttime, the wall lined with torches—too many torches, all lit up, flickering. In the room stood a sole figure, standing on the window ledge, his back to her. She sensed immediately that it was her father. He wore his royal furs, and, on his head, the crown. It seemed bigger than it had ever been.

"Father?" she asked, as she approached.

Slowly, he turned and looked at her. She was horrified. His face was half-skeleton, eyes bulging from the sockets, flesh decomposed. He looked at her with a look of horror, of desperation, as he reached out one hand.

"Why won't you avenge me?" he moaned.

Gwen's breath caught in her chest, horrified as she rushed towards him.

He started to lean back, and she reached out to grab his hand—but it was too late. He fell slowly, backwards, out the window.

Gwen shrieked as she ran forward, and stuck her head out to watch. Her father plummeted down into the blackness, falling and falling. The ground gave way, and he seemed to fall into the bowels of the earth. She never heard him hit.

Gwen heard a rattling noise, and turned and surveyed his empty chamber. There was his crown. It must have fallen off his head, and now it rolled, on its side, across the floor, making a hollow, metallic sound as it did. It rolled in circles, louder and louder, until it finally settled down. It sat there, in the center of the bare stone floor.

From somewhere, his words rang out again:

"Avenge me!"

Gwen woke with a start, sitting upright in bed, breathing hard. She rubbed her eyes and jumped from the mattress, hurrying over to her window, trying to shake herself of the awful nightmare. She took cold water from a small bowl by the window, splashed it on her face several times, and looked out.

It was dawn, and King's Court was quiet, the light just beginning to break from the first rising sun. It looked like she was the first one to rise. The dream had been awful, more like a vision, and her heart pounded as she replayed it. Thor, dying on that ship. It had felt like a message, more like she was seeing the future than a dream. Her heart broke, as she felt with certainty that he would soon be dead.

And then here was that awful image of her father, the decomposed skeleton. His rebuke to her. The images were all so real, she could not go back to sleep. She paced her chamber and hardly knew what to do with herself.

Without thinking, she crossed her room and began to dress, way earlier than usual. She felt she had to do something. Anything. Whatever she could to find her father's killer.

*

As he walked down the empty castle corridors in the early morning light, Godfrey was sober and alone—both for the first time in years—and it was an unfamiliar feeling. He could not remember how long it had been since he had gone a full day without a drink, or had spent time alone, not surrounded by his drunken friends. His feelings of loneliness, of gravity, were all new to him, and he realized that this is what everyday people must feel like as they lived their normal lives. It was terrible. Boring. He hated it, and he wanted to run back to the alehouse, to his friends, and make it all go away. Real life was not for him.

But for the first time in his life, Godfrey refused to give into his impulses. He did not know what was overcoming him, but watching his father being lowered into the earth had done something to him; since his death, something had stirred inside him. He was like a cauldron simmering on a low flame; he felt a sense of discontent, of unease, that he never had before. He felt uncomfortable in his own skin. For the first time he turned a harsh light upon himself, reevaluated who he was, how he had lived his life, and how he might spend the rest of it, and when he looked, honestly, in the mirror, he did not like what he saw.

Godfrey also looked upon his friends with fresh eyes, and could no longer stand the site of their faces. Most of all, his own. For the first time this morning, the taste of ale was rotten to him; for the first time in as long as he could remember, he had a clear head, a presence of mind. He needed to think clearly today, to summon all his wits. Because there was something burning inside him, something he did not fully understand, which was driving him to find his father's murderer.

Perhaps it was his own guilt that drove him, his unresolved relationship with his father; in some ways, he saw this as his chance to, finally, gain his father's approval. If he could not have it in life, perhaps he could gain it in death. And if he found his father's killer, he might also vindicate himself, vindicate what had been thus far of his life.

Godfrey burned, too, with the injustice of it all. He hated the idea of his brother, Gareth, sitting on the throne. Gareth had always been a scheming, manipulative human being, a cold bastard, with no love for anyone but himself. Godfrey had been around shady types all his life, and he could spot one a mile away. He recognized it in Gareth's eyes, the evil welling up and shining like something from beneath the earth. This was a man who wanted power; who wanted to dominate others. Godfrey knew that Gareth was dirty. And he felt certain that he had something to do with their father's murder.

Godfrey climbed another flight of steps, turned down a corridor, and felt himself grow cold as he walked down the final corridor leading to his father's chamber. Walking down it brought back memories, too fresh, of the approach to his father's chamber; of being summoned by him, chastised by him. He had always hated walking down this final stretch to his chamber.

Yet now, oddly, it brought forth a different sensation: it was like walking the hall of a ghost. He could almost feel his father's presence lingering here with each step he took.

Godfrey reached the last door, and turned and stood before it. It was a large, arched door, a foot thick, and looked a thousand years old. He wondered how many MacGils had used this door. It was strange to see it here like this, unguarded. Not once in Godfrey's life had he seen it without guards before it. It was as if, now, no one cared that his father had ever existed.

The door was closed, and Godfrey reached out and grasped its iron handle and pushed it open. It opened within an ancient creak, and he stepped inside.

It was even more eerie in here, in this empty chamber, which still hummed with his father's vitality. The bed was still made, his father's clothes still draped across it, his mantle still hung in the far corner, his boots by the fireplace. The window was open, a sudden summer breeze rushed in, and Godfrey felt a chill; he felt his father standing there, right with him. The breeze billowed the linens hanging over the four-poster bed, and he could not but help think it was his father speaking to him. Godfrey felt overwhelmed with sadness.

Gareth walked the room, feeling a chill as he realized this is where his father was murdered. He did not know what he was looking for exactly, but he sensed that here, where it happened, would be the place to start. Perhaps there was some small clue overlooked that could help spark an idea. He assumed that the council had already combed over this room. But he wanted to try. He *needed* to try, for himself.

But after minutes of scouring, he saw no clues that jumped out at him.

"Godfrey?" came a woman's voice.

Godfrey spun, caught off guard, not expecting anyone else in here with him. He saw, standing there, his younger sister, Gwendolyn.

"You scared me," he said, and breathed. "I did not know anyone was in here with me."

"I'm sorry," she said, stepping in and closing the door behind her. "The door was open. I did not expect to find you in here, either."

He narrowed his eyes, studying her. She looked lost, troubled.

"What are you doing here?" he asked.

"I could ask you the same," she responded. "It's too early in the day. You must have been driven here. Like myself."

Godfrey looked in all directions, looking for signs of anyone watching or listening. He realized how paranoid he had become. Slowly, warily, he nodded back.

Godfrey had always cared for Gwen. Of all his siblings, she was the only one that he felt did not judge her. He'd always appreciated how sensitive and compassionate she was. He had always sensed that, of all of his family members, she might be the only one willing to believe in him, to give him a second chance. And he felt he could tell her anything without fear of reprisal.

"You are right," he responded. "I do feel driven to be here. In fact, I can think of little else."

"I feel the same," she said. "His death was too sudden. And too violent. I find it hard to relax, to enjoy life, until I know we've caught his murderer. I had a terrible dream. And it drove me here."

Godfrey nodded. He understood.

He watched Gwendolyn as she walked about the room, taking it all in. He could see the anguish in her face, and he realized how painful this must be for her, too. After all, she was closest to their father. Closer than any of them.

"I thought that perhaps by coming here I might find something," Godfrey said, as he walked about the room again himself, looking through every corner, under the bed, through every detail. "But nothing is apparent."

She surveyed the room herself, walking slowly.

"What of these stains?" she asked.

He turned and hurried over to where she was looking. On the floor, against the dark stone, there was the faintest outline of a stain. They walked towards the window, following the trail, and as they entered the sunlight, he could see it more clearly: a bloodstain. He felt a chill. The stains covered the floors, the walls, and he realized they were his father's.

"It must have been a violent struggle," she said, following the trail throughout the room.

"Awful," he said.

"I don't know exactly what I was hoping to find here," she said. "But I think perhaps it was a waste of time. I see nothing."

"Nor do I," Godfrey said.

"Perhaps there are better places to look," she said.

"Where?"

She shrugged. "Wherever it is, it's not here."

Godfrey felt another cold breeze, and felt a chill that would not leave him. He was overcome with a desire to leave this room, and he could see in Gwen's eyes that she felt the same.

As one, they turned and headed for the door.

But as Godfrey was heading towards the door, suddenly something caught his eye that made him stop.

"Wait," he said. "Look here."

Gwen turned and looked, following him as he walked several steps across the room, towards the fireplace. He reached up, and fingered a blood stain on the wall.

"This stain, it's not like the others," he said. "It's in a different part of the room. And it's lighter."

They exchanged a puzzled look as they both examined the wall more closely.

"It could be from the murder weapon," he added. "Maybe he tried to hide it in the wall."

Godfrey touched the stones, feeling for a loose one, but he could not find it. Then Gwen stopped and pointed towards the fireplace.

"There," she said.

He looked, but did not see anything.

"Beside the fireplace pit. Do you see it? That hole in the wall. It's a chute. A waste chute."

"What of it?" he asked.

"Those stains, from the dagger. They surround it. Look at the ceiling of the pit."

They got down on their knees and looked closely, and he was amazed to realize that she was right. The stains led right to the chute.

"The dagger came this way," she deduced. "He must have thrown it down the chute."

They both turned and looked at each other, and knew where they had to go.

"The waste room," he said.

*

Godfrey and Gwendolyn wound their way down the castle's narrow stone, spiral staircase, deeper and deeper into the bowels of the castle, deeper in fact than Godfrey had ever been. Just as he was beginning to get dizzy, they reached an iron door. He turned to Gwen.

"This looks like the servants' quarters," he said. "I assume the waste room is behind these doors."

"Try it," she said.

Godfrey reached up and slammed on the door, and after a wait, he heard footsteps. Finally, the door opened. A long, solemn face stared back blankly.

"Yes?" asked the older man, clearly a lifelong servant.

Godfrey turned to Gwen, and she nodded back.

"Is this the waste room?" he asked.

"Yes," the man answered. "And also the prep room for the kitchen. What business have you here?"

Before Godfrey could respond, the man narrowed his eyes, looking at them with sudden recognition.

"Wait a moment," he added. "Are you the king's children?" His eyes lit up in deference. "You are," he answered himself. "What are you doing down here?"

"Please," Gwen said softly, stepping forward and placing a hand on his wrist. "Let us in."

The man stepped back and opened the door wide, and they hurried inside.

Godfrey was surprised by this room he had never been in, although it was in the structure he had lived in all his life. They were all in the bowels of the castle, in a vast room, dark, lit by sporadic torches, filled with burning fire pits, with wood prep tables, and huge bubbling cauldrons hanging over pits. Clearly this room was mean to hold dozens of servants. But other than this man, it was empty.

"You've come at an odd time of day," the man said. "We have not yet begun the breakfast preparations. The others will arrive shortly."

"That's OK," Godfrey answered. "We are here for another reason."

"Where is the waste pit?" Gwen asked, wasting no time.

The man stared back, baffled.

"The waste pit?" he echoed. "But why would you want to know this?"

"Please, just show it to us," Godfrey said.

The servant stared back, with his long face and sunken cheeks, then finally turned and led them across the room.

They all stopped before a large, stone pit, inside of which was an immense cauldron, one so large it needed to be hoisted by at least two people, and which looked as if it could contain the waste of the entire castle. It sat beneath a chute, which must have led high above. Godfrey could smell it from here, and he recoiled.

Godfrey stepped forward with Gwen and carefully examined the wall surrounding it. But despite their best efforts, they could see no stains, and nothing out of place.

They looked down into the cauldron, but it was empty.

"You'll find nothing in there," the servant said. "It's emptied every hour. On the hour."

Godfrey wondered if this was all a waste of time. He sighed, and he and Gwen exchanged a disappointed look.

"Is this about my master?" the attendant finally asked, breaking the silence.

"Your master?" Gwen asked.

"The one who is missing?"

"Missing?" Godfrey asked.

The servant nodded.

"He disappeared one night and never came back to work. There are rumors of a murder."

Godfrey and Gwen exchanged a look.

"Tell us more," Gwen prodded.

Before he could respond, a rear door opened, on the far side of the chamber, and in walked a man whose appearance stunned Godfrey. He was short, and wide, and most strikingly, his back was deformed, twisted and hunched over. He walked with a limp, and it was an effort for him to lift his head. He ambled over, their way.

The man finally stood before them, looking back and forth between Godfrey and the servant.

"It is a privilege that you should grace us with your presence, my lords," the hunchback said with a bow.

"Steffen would know far more about the matter than I," the other servant added, accusingly. Clearly this servant did not like Steffen.

With that, the servant turned and hurried off, crossing the room and disappearing through a back door. Steffen watched him go.

Godfrey and Gwen exchanged a look.

"Steffen, may we speak with you?" Gwen asked, softly, trying to set him at ease.

Steffen stared back at them with twisting hands, looking very nervous.

"I don't know what he told you, but that one is full of lies. And gossip," Steffen said, already defensive. "I have done nothing."

"We never said you did," Godfrey said, also trying to reassure him. It was clear that Steffen had something to hide, and he wanted to know what it was. He felt that it had something to do with his father's death.

"We want to ask you about our father, the king," Gwen said. "About the night he died. Do you recall anything unusual that night? A weapon falling down the waste chute?"

Steffen squirmed, looking at the floor, not meeting their eyes.

"I know nothing of any dagger," he said.

"Who said anything of a dagger?" Godfrey prodded.

Steffen looked back up guiltily, and Godfrey knew they had caught him in a lie. This man definitely had something to hide. He felt emboldened.

Steffen said nothing in response, but merely toed the floor, continuing to wring his hands.

"I know nothing," he repeated. "I didn't do anything wrong."

Godfrey and Gwen exchanged a knowing look. They had found someone important. Yet it was also clear he would give them nothing more. Godfrey felt that he had to do something to get him to talk.

Godfrey stepped forward, reached up, and lay a firm hand on Steffen's shoulder. Steffen looked up, guiltily, like a schoolboy who had been caught, and Godfrey scowled down, tightening his grip and holding it there.

"We know about what happened to your master," he said, bluffing. "Now, you can either tell us all we want to know about our father's murder, or we can have you thrown in the dungeon to never see light again. The choice is yours."

As he stood there, Godfrey felt the strength of his father overcome him, felt, for the first time, the inherent strength that ran in his own blood, the blood of a long line of kings. For the first time in his life, he felt strong. Confident. Worthy. He felt like a MacGil. And for once, he felt his father's approval.

Steffen must have sensed it. Because finally, after a very long while, he stopped squirming. He looked up, met Godfrey's eyes, and nodded in acquiescence.

"I won't go to jail?" he asked. "If I tell you?"

"You will not," Godfrey answered. "As long as you had nothing to do with our father's death. This I promise you."

Steffen licked his lips, thinking, then finally, after a long while, he nodded.

"OK," he finally said. "I will tell you everything."

CHAPTER TWENTY TWO

Thor sat deep in the boat, lined up with the others on the long wooden benches, both hands on the thick wooden oar as he rowed, Krohn sitting at his feet. He sweated beneath the sun, as he had for days and, breathing hard, wondered when this would ever end. The journey felt endless. At first, their sails had carried them, but then the wind had died abruptly, and all of the boys on the ship had been set to the task of rowing.

Thor sat there, somewhere in the middle of the long and narrow boat, Reese behind him and O'Connor in front, and wondered how much more of this they could stand. He had never engaged in such hard labor for so long, and every muscle in his body shook. His shoulders, wrists, forearms, biceps, his back, his neck and even his thighs—they all felt as if they would give out. His hands trembled, and his palms were raw. A few of the other Legion had already collapsed in exhaustion. This island, whatever it was they were going, felt as if it were on the far side of the world. He prayed for wind.

They were only given a brief break at nighttime, allowed to sleep for just fifteen minute shifts, while others relieved them. As he had lay there in the boat in the black of night, with Krohn curled up beside him, it had been the blackest and clearest night he had ever seen, the entire world filled with sparkling red and yellow stars; luckily, the summer weather had held, and it had not been too cold. The moist breezes of the ocean had cooled him and he had fallen asleep in moments—only to be awakened minutes later. He wondered if this was part of The Hundred, if this was their way of beginning to break them.

He was seriously starting to wonder what else lay in store for them, and whether he could handle it. His stomach growled; last night he had been given tack, a small strip of salted beef, and a small flask of rum to wash it down. He had given half of it to Krohn, who chewed it in one bite then immediately whined for more. Thor felt terrible he had no more to give him. But he hadn't had a good meal in days himself, and he was already starting to miss the comforts of home.

"How much longer will this go on?" Thor heard a boy, a couple of years older than he, call out to another boy.

"Long enough to kill us all," another boy called out, breathing hard.

"You've been to the island before," one boy called out to another, an older one, who sat there rowing, somber. "How long until we reach it? How far are we?"

The older boy, tall, muscle-bound, shrugged.

"Hard to say," he said. "We haven't even reached the rain wall yet."

"Rain wall?" the other boy called out.

But the big boy, breathing hard, fell silent again, and the ship slipped back into silence. All Thor could hear, incessantly, was the sound of oars hitting water.

Thor looked down for the millionth time, squinting against the glare of the sun, and marveled at the yellow color of the water. It was clear in places, especially close to the surface, and as he looked, he saw several exotic sea creatures swimming alongside the boat, trailing them, as if trying to keep up. He saw a long, purple snake, nearly the length of the boat, with a dozen heads on it, spaced out all along its body. As they went, its heads extended from the body, up into the open air, razor-sharp teeth opening and closing. Thor could not imagine what it was doing. Was it breathing? Was it trying to catch some insects in the air? Or was it threatening them?

Thor could hardly imagine what sort of strange creatures lay in store where they were going. He tried not to think about it. It was a different part of the world, and anything was possible. Would that be part of the training? He had a sinking feeling that it would.

One of the boys, a tall, frail boy who Thor recognized from the playing fields, suddenly leaned over on his oar and collapsed, about ten feet away. He slumped sideways, then fell with a thud onto the wooden floor. It was the boy from the exercise with the shields, the one who had been afraid to do it, who had been made to run extra laps. Thor had felt bad for him; he still did.

Without thinking, Thor stopped rowing, jumped from his seat and rushed to his side. He was dimly aware that it was against the rules for him to leave his seat, but he just reacted, seeing his fellow Legion member in trouble. He turned him over, looked at his face. His face was too red, his skin burnt from the sun, and his lips too dry and chapped. He was alive, but his breathing was shallow.

"Get up!" Thor urged, shaking him.

The boy's eyes fluttered.

"I can't do it anymore," he answered weakly.

"Get up!" Thor whispered urgently. "Get up quickly! Before they see you!"

"THORGRIN!" screamed Kolk.

Thor felt a hard boot kick in the small of his back, and went flying forward, face first, onto the floor of the boat. The wood stung his face and palms as he hit.

"WHAT DO YO THINK YOU'RE DOING!?"

Thor was indignant, red-faced with rage, but he held himself from doing anything rash. He turned and looked up.

"He collapsed!" Thor protested. "I was just helping—"

"You NEVER leave your seat! For ANY reason! We don't baby each other here. If he falls, let him fall!" Kolk screamed, standing over Thor, hands on his hips. Thor felt a fresh hatred for the man. What stung more than the kick was being yelled at in front of the other boys. It hurt his pride, and Thor vowed revenge. Sometimes, as a commander, Kolk was just too harsh.

Krohn came running to his side, and snarled back at Kolk.

At the site of him, Kolk seemed to be wary of coming any closer. Instead, he pointed a shaking finger towards his seat.

"Now get back there!" he screamed, "Or I'll throw you off this boat myself!"

Thor rose to one knee, when suddenly he spotted something over Kolk's shoulder that made him freeze.

"LOOK OUT!" Thor screamed, pointing.

Kolk spun, but it was already too late. Thor had no choice: he dove forward, and tackled Kolk, knocking him down to the ground—and just in time.

A split second later there was a resounding boom, and a cannonball came flying through the air, right for them. It soared across the deck of the ship, just passing where Kolk had been standing; it nearly grazed his head as he hit the deck. It singed the top railing, and there was the sound of wood splintering; miraculously, it did not do serious damage to the ship, as the cannonball sailed by and landed with a huge splash in the water.

Because of Thor's warning, all the other Legion members ducked just in time. As one, they, on the floor, raised their heads and looked out.

There, on the horizon, rowing towards them, was a huge black ship. It sailed with a yellow flag, with an emblem of a black shield in its center, two horns protruding from it.

"Empire ship!" Kolk screamed.

It was closing in fast, its large cannon pointed right at them, and manned with at least a hundred soldiers. The ships were unequally matched: theirs was larger, had a cannon, and was packed with more soldiers. Worse, their ship was manned with Empire savages—huge, overflowing with muscles, with red skin and horns sticking from their bald heads, large yellow eyes, a small triangle for noses, and impossibly wide jaws, with rows of razor-sharp teeth, and two large fangs sticking out on either end. They were formidable creatures, and they stood on the deck, wielding swords and salivating at the sight of their ship.

"MAN THE GALLEYS!" Kolk screamed, regaining his feet.

The boys broke into action. Thor hardly knew what was happening, or what he was supposed to do, but the older boys seemed to fall into place.

"ARCHERS TO THE FRONT!" Kolk screamed. "Prepare your arrows! All others set the arrows aflame!"

All around Thor, the older boys, more disciplined, hurried forward to the edge of the ship as they grabbed bows and arrows from racks off the side of the ship. The younger Legion members raced to their side, grabbing rags, dipping them in oil, wrapping them onto the end of the arrows, and lighting them on fire.

Thor wanted to help. He saw an archer kneeling, with no one helping him, and he rushed into action. He ran to his side, dipped a rag in oil, tied it to his arrow, and lit it as he placed it on the string. The boy immediately pulled back and fired, as did dozens of others around him.

The arrows, alight with flames, sailed through the air; most fell short, hissing as they landed in the sea, while about a dozen of them landed on the enemy ship. But they landed on the decks, falling short of the huge canvas sails, missing their marks. The savages, well-trained, immediately pounced on them and put them out. The first volley had done no damage.

The Empire, on the other hand, adjusted its cannon and fired again.

"DOWN!" screamed Kolk.

Thor, heart pounding, hit the deck face first with all the others—and pulled Krohn down with him. There came another boom, and another cannonball went flying past—again grazing the ship, though this time, with a cracking noise, it managed to take out a good chunk of the railing, wood splintering and sending it like missiles over Thor's head.

"BACK TO THE BOWS!" Kolk yelled.

The archers took their places again, and Thor rushed over to help, lighting an arrow and handing it to an archer, who immediately placed it on the string and let it fly. The boat was closer, and this time they had more luck. The Empire ship, fearless, came in fast, not worried about closing the gap, hardly fifty yards away. They must have figured they could overtake them so quickly, the arrows would do no harm.

That was their big mistake. This time, several dozen of the flaming arrows hit the sails; while the savages put some of them out, enough of them caught. In moments, their sails were in flames.

"GET DOWN!" Kolk yelled.

Thor looked up just in time to see the savages standing on the edge of the railing, holding huge spears, and throwing them right at their ship.

Thor dove down, pulling Krohn, his heart pounding, as spears whizzed through the air all around him and he heard them puncturing the wood.

He heard a scream, and turned to see one of his brothers, an older boy he did not know, scream out, clutching his arm, punctured by a spear and gushing blood. Thor quickly surveyed the others and saw that, luckily, none of the others seemed badly hurt, or worse, dead. Most had managed to take cover in time.

Thor looked back up and saw the Empire ship was even closer. Now maybe thirty yards away, he could see the yellows of the savages' eyes. Their ship was engulfed in flames, but their warriors seemed hardly to care. They were rowing twice as hard, preoccupied with reaching their ship and apparently, taking it over. Krohn barked and snarled at the foreign ship.

"THE SPEARS!" Kolk yelled, as he ran over and grabbed one himself. "HURL THEM BACK!"

All around Thor the boys jumped into action, hurrying over to grab the spears stuck in the wood. Thor rushed over and grabbed one himself, yanking it out of the wood. It was thick and long and was stuck surprisingly deep; it took all his might to get it out.

But he did. He ran to the edge of the ship, and surveyed his target. Beside him, Reese and Elden hurled spears, and Thor watched as they fell short, landing in the water. All around him the boys spears fell short. Very few hit the ship, and those that did missed their targets.

Thor set his sights on a single, thick rope, high up on the enemy ship, holding the main mast in place. He closed his eyes and focused, feeling an energy rise up within him, feeling his body grow warm. He tried to let his energy force take over, guide him, control him.

Thor took several steps forward, leaned back, and hurled the spear through the air.

He watched as it went flying, and felt a swell of pride as he sensed that it was on course.

It was a perfect strike.

The spear sliced the main rope in half, and it snapped with a resounding noise. As it did, their burning sail began to topple, then came crashing down, landing vertically across the ship, and engulfing the entire deck in flames.

Screams rang out from the savages, as many were caught on fire. Moments later their ship started rocking violently, and then it turned sideways and capsized, bodies jumping off into the water.

The Legion members let out a shout, victorious, and Thor wondered if anyone had seen the throw that he'd made.

"Nice one," someone said, and a boy he did not recognize patted him on the back.

Thor turned and saw others looking at him in admiration, and he felt his pride swell. He felt a sense of victory. He had at first been terror-stricken stricken to see that Empire ship, to realize they were really in hostile territory. But now that they had defeated it, he felt that anything was possible. He felt that, if they could withstand this, they could withstand anything.

Just then, there came a shout: "EMPIRE FLEET!"

Thor looked up and saw one of the Legion high up on the mast, looking out and pointing at the horizon.

Thor ran to the railing with the others and looked out. His heart dropped: there, on the horizon, sat an entire fleet of Empire ships.

Thor's heart pounded in his chest. There was no way they could defeat this many ships. And no way they could escape back to the Ring in time. They were finished.

"THE RAIN WALL!" someone else yelled out.

Thor turned in the other direction, and saw, on the horizon, what looked like a wall of water. It was unlike anything he had ever seen. It was a perfectly clear day, clear skies all around them—and yet, on the horizon there sat a straight wall of rain. It didn't move, but just sat there, like a waterfall in the middle of nowhere.

"What is it?" Thor asked Reese, standing beside them.

"It's the boundary to the other side. To the Dragon's Sea."

"TO THE OARS! ROW FOR THE RAIN WALL!" Kolk yelled, frantically. It was the first time Thor heard fear in his voice.

Thor raced back to his spot, rowing with all he had, as did everyone around him. Their ship started moving quickly, right for the wall, and as they got closer, strong current sucked them in, towards it, like a whirlpool. Thor looked back and saw the Empire ships bearing down on them.

"And what of the Empire ships?" Thor called out to Reese.

Reese, in front of him, shook his head.

"They won't follow. Not through the rain wall."

"But why?" Thor asked.

"It's too dangerous. They wouldn't risk it. Beyond that wall, there lies a sea of monsters."

Thor looked down at the water, and wondered.

"But if it's too dangerous for them, what hope is there for us?"

Reese shook his head.

"It's the only way. We have no choice."

As they neared the rain wall Thor heard the great roar of water hitting water, felt the spray even from here, and looked back to see the Empire ships had stopped the chase.

Thor felt relieved to be rid of them, but scared for what lay before them. Krohn whined. As Thor's body became doused in freezing water, as his world became a blur, he grabbed onto the mast for dear life, as did all the other boys around him. In moments he was doused with water, spraying down so hard it sent him flying across the ship. He tried to grab on, but he could not, as he lost his grip and slipped all the way across the deck. Water filled his eyes, his ears, his nose, and as he reached out, flailing, as he tried to breathe, water filling his lungs, he could not help but wonder: if these waters were too dangerous for the Empire, what sort of creatures could possibly lie beyond?

COMING SOON....
Book #3 in the Sorcerer's Ring

About Morgan Rice

Morgan Rice is the #1 Bestselling author of THE VAMPIRE JOURNALS, a young adult series comprising eight books, which has been translated into six languages.

Morgan is also author of the #1 Bestselling THE VAMPIRE LEGACY, a young adult series comprising two books and counting.

Morgan is also author of the #1 Bestselling ARENA ONE and ARENA TWO, the first two books in THE SURVIVAL TRILOGY, a post-apocalyptic action thriller set in the future.

Morgan loves to hear from you, so please feel free to visit www.morganricebooks.com to stay in touch.

Books by Morgan Rice

THE SURVIVAL TRILOGY
ARENA ONE (BOOK #1)
ARENA TWO (BOOK #2)

the Vampire Legacy
resurrected (book #1)
craved (book #2)

the Vampire Journals
turned (book #1)
loved (book #2)
betrayed (book #3)
destined (book #4)
desired (book #5)
betrothed (book #6)
vowed (book #7)
found (book #8)

CPSIA information can be obtained at www.ICGtesting.com
Printed in the USA
LVOW08s1425010913

350471LV00001B/89/P